+

W737m   Winthrop, Elizabeth
Miranda in the middle.

ELIZABETH WINTHROP

Miranda in the Middle

HOLIDAY HOUSE
New York

For my brothers, Nicky and Andrew,

because, of all my characters,

Miranda is their favorite

Library of Congress Cataloging in Publication Data

Winthrop, Elizabeth.
  Miranda in the middle.

  SUMMARY: Miranda finds herself on the spot with
her best friend and also with a new friend she meets
while running. Sequel to Marathon Miranda.
  [1. Friendship—Fiction] I. Title.
PZ7.W768Mi   [Fic]   80-15847
ISBN 0-8234-0422-6

Contents

1 · Alex Finds His Subject

"Shall we go back up to Ninety-third Street?" Phoebe asked.

I rolled my eyeballs. We had already run two miles. "Who do you think I am?" I gasped. "How about Eighty-eighth Street?"

Phoebe nodded. She wasn't going to waste her breath talking. She upped the pace a bit, but I didn't try to keep up with her. We had been running together too long to bother racing with each other. When I'd tried it last year, all I'd gotten was a big asthma attack and a trip to the hospital.

I whistled for Frisbee, my dog, when I turned the corner and headed up the hill to the Monument. She came loping up behind me. We waited at the top for Phoebe. Pretty soon I saw her coming along the sidewalk.

There was a tall blond guy running beside her and

when she slowed down, she waved at him. "Goodbye," she said. "See you again."

"Sure," he said and went loping past.

"Who was that?" I asked.

"I don't know his name," Phoebe said. "He started talking to me down by the playground. He wanted to know where I bought my shoes."

I burst out laughing, and Phoebe looked a little hurt. "That's some line," I said. "Everybody knows you can get those shoes anywhere on Broadway."

"Maybe he's new to the neighborhood." She shrugged. "Anyway, he seemed nice."

"Didn't your mother ever warn you about talking to strangers?" I asked as we crossed the street.

"If I'd listened to her, I never would have met you," she said. We both smiled. Phoebe picked me up in the park last year because our dogs looked like twins. Then she convinced me to start running, and one thing led to another. Now we're best friends. And so are our dogs. Except Dungeon isn't Phoebe's dog. He belongs to the Fosters, who live across the hall from her. They pay Phoebe to walk him. With all the running she does, the Fosters sure are getting their money's worth.

"Want to come up?" I asked.

"Sure. I'm always interested in Alex's latest observation on the world."

Alex is my brother. He can't decide whether he

wants to be a psychiatrist or a gym teacher. Since he's not old enough to do either, he practices on me. If he's not analyzing my every move, he's showing me some great new exercise he learned from his friend Peter. Peter wants to be a weight lifter. As Phoebe once said, that's lucky, because he doesn't have any extra brains to throw around.

"Alex might not be in," I said as we waited for the elevator. "He's enrolled himself in some new calisthenics course at the Y."

"Trust Alex," Phoebe said. "Even I think he goes a little overboard."

But he was in. Sitting at the dining room table eating a bowl of granola. Naturally.

"Hello, runners. I saw you two down there. How many miles did you do?"

"Three or four," Phoebe said. "Yuk. That looks like baby food."

"I mashed some banana in it," Alex said. "Very high on potassium."

"Want some ice cream, Phoebe?" I asked. She nodded.

I dished it up and signaled to her to follow me. I wasn't up to one of Alex's lectures on the various ways ice cream rots your stomach. He's also a health food nut.

We stepped over our two dogs and settled down on my bed with our backs against the wall.

"How do you like having your own room?" Phoebe asked. "I haven't been over since your father put up the partition."

"It's great. Even though the room is half its old size, I don't have to trip over Alex's weight-lifting equipment and his psychology books. Plus I got the view." My window looks north right up the Hudson River to the George Washington Bridge.

"How'd you get Alex to agree to that?" Phoebe asked.

"We drew straws and I won. Anyway, his window looks east into the city so he gets the morning light. Besides, he got a pair of binoculars for his birthday, so he spends his time watching the people who live in the brownstones on that block and making notes on them. Little do they know their fate."

Phoebe laughed. "They'll probably end up in some study on how people behave in brownstones."

We were quiet for a minute. One of the nice things about good friends is you don't have to talk all the time when you're with them.

"How are your parents?" I asked.

Phoebe shrugged. "Same as always. I still see that doctor on the East Side on Wednesday afternoons, but I think they're the ones who should be seeing him, not me."

"I thought they were."

"They stopped after about a month. My father was brought up to believe that psychiatrists are unnecessary and shouldn't be trusted. Alex should go talk to him sometime." Phoebe jumped up and went to the window. She lives right across the street in a big apartment building and she has her own room, but it doesn't have a river view. Last summer, Phoebe found out she was adopted. It really hit her hard. I don't blame her. It would make me feel strange to find out suddenly that my parents had been keeping this big secret from me for my whole life, thirteen years.

"I'd better go. I've got a history test tomorrow," she said. "Come on, Dungeon." Dungeon raised his head, looked at her, and put it down again.

"I think you're running that poor dog into an early grave," I said.

Phoebe looked worried. "The Fosters are talking about giving him to some friend in New Jersey. I'll have to convince Mother to let me have him."

"I thought your parents wouldn't let you have a dog."

"That was last year. I can always try again."

"See you tomorrow at the usual time?" I asked.

"Right. We might try going over to Central Park. I'm getting a little bored with Riverside Park. Come on, Dungeon." This time he got up and went. Frisbee didn't even lift her head to say good-bye. Rude dog.

When I went back to the kitchen, I saw my mother had left me a note. It was my year to "stuff the windows." The wind off the Hudson River is so strong in the winter that the old windows in our apartment rattle and let in the cold air. Every year, in the fall, we stuff them with foam strips. It's a very boring job which requires standing on the radiator covers and poking the foam into the crack with a dull knife. I was right in the middle of it when Alex came in behind me. I didn't hear him, so the sound of his voice almost made me fall off the radiator.

"I have found him," he said in this graveyard voice.

"Who?" I shrieked, clinging to the curtain.

"My subject," Alex said. He settled himself down at the dining room table. "Medium height, brown hair, slim build, given to wearing frayed blue jeans and a black leather jacket, basketball sneakers."

"What are you talking about?"

"Miranda, sometimes you can be so dense. Remember I told you I had to do a special project for my independent study this fall? Well, I've picked the person I'm going to study. He sits outside his window on the fire escape and watches the church next door."

"What do you mean, he watches the church?" I asked, poking fiercely at a bumpy piece of foam.

"Just what I said. Every afternoon, he's sitting out there, staring at the church through his binoculars."

"Maybe he's planning to rob the poor box," I volunteered. I thought that was quite a brilliant suggestion.

"Miranda, it's a Methodist church. They don't have poor boxes."

Oops, wrong again.

"I don't know, Alex. I don't think staring at a church through your binoculars is any stranger than staring at some poor unsuspecting victim. Maybe somebody should use you for their independent study project." Alex was glaring at me. Without even turning around, I could feel his eyeballs boring into my back.

"Miranda, you don't understand anything about the study of science. Observation of human behavior is fundamental to psychology."

He went blabbing on, but I tuned out. When Alex starts lecturing, you just have to rise above him, as my father says. When I try to argue with Alex, I get madder and madder and he gets calmer and more patronizing. That's his way of practicing for his great future as the next Dr. Freud.

I stuffed in the last piece of foam and climbed down from the window. Alex had stopped talking. He was scribbling notes in his pad. Another revolting habit of his. I tried to peer nonchalantly over his shoulder but no such luck. He slipped the pad back into his pocket just as I had gotten into position. He keeps his notebooks in a locked drawer in his desk. Someday I'm going to break in and steal them.

The front door slammed.

"Anybody home?" my mother called.

"We're in the dining room," I answered.

"I remembered everything today," she said proudly as she put the grocery bag down on the kitchen counter. "We're having spaghetti."

"Meat," Alex barked.

"Here."

"Spaghetti."

"Here."

"Mushrooms, tomato sauce, onions."

"Here, here, here!" Mother shouted, slamming them down on the counter.

"Congratulations," I said, thumping her on the back. "It's a first."

"Not exactly," Mother reminded me. "I remember I did it once last spring. I think it was in March . . ." Her voice drifted off and the three of us had a good laugh. My mother has a well-deserved reputation for being vague.

"How was work?" I asked.

She rolled her eyes to heaven. "I had to fire two maids today. A guest caught them stealing her clothes." My mother works in the personnel office at the Sheraton Hotel. Never a dull moment there. I keep telling Alex that's where he should do his research.

"How about you two? How was school?"

"Same old stuff," I said. "Phoebe and I ran three miles today. I'm going to take a shower."

"About time," Alex muttered.

As I walked by, I gave him a sharp rap on the top of the head.

"Ouch," he yelled.

"That's what Japanese mothers do when their children misbehave," I called over my shoulder. "I read about it in my anthropology course. It's called conditioning."

"You don't take anthropology," I heard him holler just before I closed the bathroom door. That Alex. Doesn't miss a trick.

2 · *Margaret and Grandpa*

The phone rang during dinner that night. It was my grandfather.

"Hello, Miranda," he said. "How are you?"

"Fine, Grandpa. How's Vermont?"

"The snow is here already. I was thinking of coming down to the sunny south to see all of you. Is your mother there?"

"Just a minute."

I handed the phone to Mother and sat back down. Now that was strange. Grandpa used to live in New York, but he moved to Vermont to get away. He hardly ever comes to the city except on vacations.

"What does Grandpa want?" Alex asked.

"He's thinking of coming to visit us," I said slowly.

"Great," Pops said. "He hasn't been here in ages."

"I bet he's coming to see Margaret," Alex said.

Of course. That was it. Last summer, when we'd

gone up to Vermont for our annual visit, we'd invited Margaret to come with us. She's this special friend of mine who lives on the third floor. She takes care of me if I come home early from school because of my asthma, and we take special trips around the city together. In fact, this Sunday, we had a plan to go to the Lower East Side.

Anyway, Margaret and Grandpa had really hit it off. She's just about his age. Phoebe and I think they might get married. Wait till I tell Phoebe Grandpa's coming down.

Mother got off the phone. "Alex, it's your night to do the dishes," she said.

"Is Grandpa coming?" I asked.

"Yes. He's arriving on the bus Friday night, and he'll go back on Monday."

"Terrific," I said.

"He's already talked to Margaret. They made a date to go out to dinner Saturday night, so I convinced him to bring her here."

"See. Just what I told you," Alex said. He stood up and started to carry the plates into the kitchen.

"Now, don't you two start badgering them," Mother said. "When you got back from Vermont in September, you practically had them married off, poor souls."

"Not a word, Mother, I promise."

I sat at the table for a long time, watching the river. There was this funny little pain deep inside me that

I couldn't quite understand. I love Grandpa and I love Margaret, but I wasn't really sure I wanted them to be together. I guess I was scared of losing them both.

"You're awfully quiet tonight," Pops said, sitting down beside me. "Waiting for the big boat?"

I shook my head. "Just thinking."

"How's the running?"

"Fine. We do about three miles a day. I hardly ever get asthma anymore. It makes me think Alex was right about it being in my head," I said in a whisper. "Don't ever tell him I said so."

Pops grinned. "Don't worry. But you should take that inhaler with you anyway. It's not all in your head, kid. You do have asthma and it gets worse in the cold weather."

"Phoebe never lets me out of the house without it. That attack last summer scared her to death."

We were quiet for a minute. Pops started sketching something on a napkin. He's a free-lance illustrator. He would really like to be an artist who could spend all day painting big abstract pictures, but he can't afford to. One day when I'm rich and famous, I'm going to give him a lot of money so he can have his own studio.

"Miranda, why don't you run downstairs and tell Margaret about Saturday night?"

"Sure."

Margaret took a long time opening the door. She

appeared with her watering can in hand. "Sorry, Miranda. I was doing the bedroom plants. Come on in."

We went back to her room and she continued the rounds while we talked. Margaret must have at least a hundred plants. She works at the Botanical Garden two afternoons a week.

"What's up? The only time I see you is if I look out the window and catch you jogging up the Promenade. You must be ready for another marathon."

I grinned. "Not yet. Phoebe probably is. It seems to me she could go about five more miles if I weren't holding her back."

Margaret bent over and peered at one of her plants. "Uh-oh."

"What's wrong?"

"Scale. Dread disease of all indoor plants. I'll have to put it in solitary confinement in the bathroom."

"Mother sent me down to tell you that she's asked you and Grandpa for dinner Saturday night, and Grandpa's accepted," I said.

"How nice," she said, poking her head out the bathroom door.

"Maybe I'll get Phoebe over and we can have a reunion," I said as we went back into the living room.

"That would be fun," Margaret said. "Now are we still on for Sunday? The Lower East Side? Tour number Forty-two B?"

"Sure," I said.

"I asked your grandfather if he wanted to come. I bet in all his stuffy Wall Street days, he never saw that part of town."

We smiled at each other. "Well, back to the math homework," I said. "See you Saturday night."

"Grandpa's coming to visit this weekend," I said to Phoebe in the bus the next morning. We ride to school together in the mornings. There usually isn't much conversation because Phoebe is always trying to finish some homework at the last minute. I don't know how she can stand to leave everything so long. She's going to get an ulcer from the tension. This time it was history, and she was concentrating so hard she didn't answer. I don't think she even heard me, but I just kept on talking anyway. "He and Margaret are having dinner with us Saturday night." I waited for a reaction. None. "They're going to get married."

Phoebe looked up. "You're kidding?"

"Yes, I am kidding. I just wanted to see if you were listening."

"Sorry, Miranda. I'm trying to write out the answers to these history questions, and people keep bumping into me."

The bus was really crowded this morning. As usual, there was one right behind us that was practically empty. My father says they should tie the buses together and save on gas. At Central Park West, people started pushing in the back door.

"Hey, we had to pay," yelled one lady. "You're cheating. Go in the front door like everybody else."

"Look, lady, it's too crowded up there. Don't hassle me."

"What a way to start your morning," I said to Phoebe. I hate scenes on the bus. They make me nervous.

"Just ignore them," Phoebe said. "We've only got two more stops."

When we got up to get off at Madison Avenue, the lady near the back door slipped and fell. She took forever to get up.

"Hey, you're taking that man's wallet," Phoebe yelled at the man next to her. He turned around and glared at Phoebe.

"What do you mean, kid? I'm just trying to help the lady here."

"You weren't either. You were taking that man's wallet," Phoebe said again. I almost died. I was sure the guy was going to knife Phoebe right there on the bus.

"The kid's right," said another man. "I saw you too. You got your wallet, mister?"

The other passenger nodded. People filed off the bus, it roared away, and there we were on the side-walk with the would-be robber. Phoebe turned away and started walking quickly, while I tried to catch up.

"Is he following us?" Phoebe asked.

I glanced back. "No, he's talking to that lady who fell down."

Phoebe nodded grimly. "Just what I thought. They're in cahoots. She did that falling act to give him time to rip somebody off. Incredible."

Well, of course, I had missed all that. "I was sure he was going to murder you. You're really brave," I said.

"To be honest with you, I didn't think about it," Phoebe said with a shrug. "The words were out of my mouth before I could stop them." She stopped. "This is where I turn. See you this afternoon in the park."

I waved good-bye. All day long, I kept thinking of what she did on the bus and wondering if I would have said anything. It worried me.

I told the story that night at dinner. "What would you've done, Pops?" I asked.

My father thought for a while. "Phoebe did a brave thing, but it was also a little foolish. If that man works the crosstown bus a lot, he may remember her. Horrible as it sounds, it may have been wiser to keep quiet."

"I wouldn't want to have anything happen to you, Miranda, over one man's wallet. You never know what these people will do," my mother said. She knew what she was talking about. After all, she has to deal with weirdos all day long.

"I would have told the bus driver about it," Alex said.

"There was no way to get to the front," I said. "The bus was packed with people. Some people had even gotten on through the back door at Central Park West." I sat back. "Wait a minute. The people who got on without paying were the same ones who tried to pull off the robbery."

"Of course they were," Alex said. "Most muggers don't pay their bus fare if they can get out of it."

Well, the whole thing taught me a lesson. I spent every morning for the next week checking every face to be sure we didn't end up on the same bus with that pair again. Phoebe seemed to have forgotten the whole thing. I can't decide whether she's brave or just stupid, but I feel it's my job to protect her.

Grandpa arrived late on Friday night. I was still awake when he came in, so I went out in my pajamas to say hello. He looked wonderful. If Margaret didn't fall in love with him, she was crazy.

"Hello, Miranda," he said, wrapping me in a wonderful bear hug that smelled of pipe smoke. "How's the marathon runner?"

"I'm fine. How's the experimental farmer?"

He grinned. "Just fine, thanks. Got a little lonely up there for all of you though. The place seemed empty after you left."

"That's because we filled it up with so many unexpected guests," Mother said. She smiled at me. Last summer, Phoebe had run away and turned up at

Grandpa's. And, of course, I had already invited Margaret.

"I hope you bring them back this summer," Grandpa said. "That place is too big for one lonely old man."

My mother and father exchanged what Alex would call a significant look. I'm sure Grandpa saw it too. There was this little silence in the room.

"Well, good night, everybody. See you tomorrow," I said as I trooped off to bed. I had the feeling that they wanted to discuss something without me around.

It was times like these that I wished Alex and I still shared a room. Sometimes you need a body around to talk to even if that person is going to try and psychoanalyze you to death. I tiptoed to his door and opened it, but the lights were out and I could hear his heavy breathing. So I went to bed and stared at the ceiling for a long time before I fell asleep.

3 · Michael Oliver Westwater

Dinner Saturday night was really fun. Phoebe joined us, and my mother made pumpkin pie, my absolutely favorite dessert. Margaret looked very pretty. She wore a long plaid skirt she made last year. I know because I helped her pick out the material. We sat around the table for hours, laughing at Grandpa's old stories we'd heard a hundred times before. For once, Mother didn't make us get up and do the dishes the minute dessert was over. She didn't even worry about the candles burning down. Usually, she hops up and blows them out as the last person puts the last bite in his mouth. Alex says it's because she worries people aren't enjoying their food so she wants the meal to be over with. I think she just doesn't like to waste candles.

The traffic on the river was busy, and every so often somebody'd stop the conversation and point out what boat was going up or down. Grandpa and Margaret didn't seem to pay any particular attention to each other, but then they must have known Phoebe and I were watching them like hawks.

Finally, Margaret got up and said it was time to go. Grandpa stood up too and suggested they go for a walk. We all laughed and off they went together. They slipped out of our grasp just like that.

"I'll walk you home, Phoebe," I said. "Be right back," I called as we went out the door.

"Did Margaret come out this way?" I asked Jimmy, the night doorman.

He nodded. "She went up the block."

"There they are," I said to Phoebe. "Let's go."

But Phoebe hung back. "Come on, Miranda. Let's leave them alone. How are they ever going to fall in love if we hang around all the time?"

I shrugged. "I'm not sure I want them to fall in love."

"Really?"

"Well, if Margaret marries Grandpa, then she'll probably move to Vermont, and I'll only see her a couple of times a year. Or if Grandpa moves down here, then we won't have the farm to go to in the summer."

We walked across the street to the lobby of Phoebe's building. Our doormen are nosier than hers.

"I see what you mean," she said. "But there isn't

anything you can do about it. Maybe they'll keep both places."

I hadn't thought of that. "That's true," I said. "Then I could have both of them for some of the time."

"Thanks for dinner. I had a great time."

"Do you want to come with us tomorrow? Margaret and I are taking Grandpa to the Lower East Side. Another one of her special tours."

"Oh, no thanks. I have to stay in and do homework."

"On a Sunday?" I asked. "You're kidding."

Phoebe shrugged and looked away. "My parents are really cracking down."

"That's too bad," I said. "See you Monday on the bus."

"Yeah, good night," she said in a distracted way as she wandered off to the elevator. I had this strange feeling there was something she wasn't telling me. But then I have a tendency to think I've been left out of things.

It was cold the next morning but clear. Grandpa, Margaret, and I met in the lobby. Grandpa had on his red plaid lumber jacket.

"My," said Margaret, "you certainly do look the picture of the Vermont farmer."

"I don't want anybody to think I have a lot of money to spend," he said, giving me a little poke with his elbow. "Onward, fearless leader."

We went downtown on the subway. By the time we got there, the streets were crowded with people pushing in and out of stores. On Orchard Street, the wares were displayed on hangers above the street. Grandpa wandered along with his mouth open.

"Look at the country bumpkin," Margaret said to me in a low voice, and we both smiled. I was getting a crick in my neck from turning around to be sure Grandpa was still in sight.

Margaret and I spent a long time in a big material store looking for new curtains for her living room. Grandpa didn't seem to mind the wait. He wandered around the aisles fingering the bolts of cloth and watching the people haggling over prices. Then we went next door and picked out a pair of boots for him. By that time, we were exhausted and ready for lunch.

"Chinatown," Margaret said. "I know just the place."

Grandpa waved her on and we followed, dodging people and cars for eight blocks or so. She led us into a little tea room which was dimly lit.

"Now," she said, "you two let me order."

"We're in your hands," Grandpa said. "But make it quick or I'll start munching on the tablecloth."

Margaret signaled to the waiter. He brought over a huge tray filled with strange-looking dishes. Margaret looked over the selection carefully and then chose about ten things. I had no idea what any of them were and said so.

"That doesn't matter," she answered. "Dig in. If you really want to know, we'll ask."

Well, even my mother would have been proud if she had seen me pile into that meal. I just closed my eyes and started munching, and to my surprise, I liked almost everything. We all ate and ate and drank tea out of little cups for what seemed like hours.

"Now, that hit the spot," Grandpa said with a contented sigh. "The body has been refueled."

"It was nice, wasn't it?" Margaret said. I could see she was pleased with herself.

"Margaret always knows the best places to eat," I said. "Next time you come, we'll take you to our place in Little Italy. Only rule is you can't tell a soul about it. We don't want it to be ruined. Right, Margaret?"

"Right." She looked at Grandpa. "Now, how about it, Kevin? Will there be a next time or have we completely put you off the city, with all this tramping around?"

He looked at her for a long time without saying anything. I felt this strange little lump in my throat, and I don't know whether it came from being happy or sad.

Finally, he cleared his throat. "Of course, there'll

be a next time, my dears." He said "dears," but he was talking to her. "I just haven't decided whether it will be your place or mine."

Well, after that moment, the afternoon didn't seem right anymore. Two's a couple, three's a crowd, or whatever that saying is. Grandpa suggested we go to Wall Street so he could show us the building he used to work in. I excused myself, saying I had a running date with Phoebe. They didn't exactly seem relieved to say good-bye to me, but they weren't bugging me to stay either. They did insist on walking me to the subway stop.

"You mean you can really get yourself home from here?" Grandpa asked.

"Sure, Grandpa," I said quite proudly.

"City kids are very independent," Margaret said, patting his arm. "Miranda's been going to school on the bus by herself since she was nine."

"Take care of yourself," he said.

"Don't worry. I'll see you tonight," I said, trying to sound cheerier than I felt.

Nobody was home when I got there, not even Frisbee. I changed into my running clothes and headed to the park to shake off these stupid left-out feelings. I ran to the track south of the boat basin and went round and round it in a kind of trance. That often happens to me when I'm running. Nothing hurts, not the breathing, not the muscles, not the feet, and I feel as if I could run forever. The afternoon sun had warmed things up just enough so I was comfortable without being hot. Round and around I went until a voice slowed me down.

"That's the first time you've ever done ten laps," the voice said from over my right shoulder. I glanced back but his face was just a bumpy blur and then he went off the track behind me. From the other half of the circle, I could see him hunched over on the side, looking at a sketch pad. What a strange kid. How did he know how many laps I'd done before?

He glanced up and waved when I went by again but I ignored him. He made me furious, breaking into my trance like that. Now I could feel my body, and it was beginning to ache. I slowed down to a walk and headed north up the path through the apple trees. Suddenly, there he was beside me again.

"Where's the dog?" he asked.

"What dog?" I asked, trying to sound nonchalant. I mean you can't trust anybody these days, not even a skinny-looking kid in glasses.

"The golden retriever. I always see you running with him."

"Her," I said shortly. "She's out." We walked along in silence for a while.

"Have you been spying on me?" I asked.

"Not exactly. I just notice things. I keep records of everything in my notebooks. See?"

He held up the pad, and I flipped through it. It was filled with all sorts of lists and sketches of buildings and notes about the weather and the time buses arrived and departed on different days. "Weird," I said as I handed it back to him. "Why do you do it?"

"I like to keep track of things," he said with a shrug. "Like your friend. The one with the dog just like yours. She was out running today with somebody else."

I looked at him sharply. "What do you mean?"

"Just what I said. She was out running with a boy." I noticed he had to scurry along to keep up with me.

"So?" I asked.

"So, nothing. Just thought you might want to know."

Well, I didn't talk to him after that. I thought if I just kept my trap shut, he'd go away.

"I live in the building next to yours. I've seen you going in and out."

I still didn't answer although I felt this little softening toward him. He seemed sort of pathetic and eager, the way he was trotting to keep up and babbling away at me.

"We don't have much of a view. Are you on the river side?"

"Yes." I couldn't help myself.

"Lucky," he said, a little spitefully. "You're probably so used to it, you don't even notice the boats."

"Oh, we do too. We keep a chart. What goes up and down and when."

Well, his whole face lit up as if I'd given him a

present. "You really do?" he said. "You're not just making fun of me?"

"No, I'm not. You aren't the only one who keeps track of things," I muttered. What a strange day this was turning out to be.

I turned up the path to the Monument but he didn't leave. Guess he was headed home too.

"What's your name?" he asked. He was panting quite heavily from the effort of keeping up with me.

"You're in terrible shape," I said. "You ought to start running."

"I hate exercise," he muttered.

I laughed in spite of myself.

He looked very hurt.

"I'm not laughing at you," I said quickly. "You just remind me of myself last year. I used to say the same thing."

"What's your name?" he asked again.

"My parents taught me never to tell anybody my name. Especially some guy who picks me up in the park."

We stopped at the curb and waited for the light. That stupid red light is never on my schedule.

"I'll tell you my name if you promise not to laugh."

I have to admit that made me curious. "All right, I promise."

"It's Michael Oliver Westwater." He flinched, waiting for the peals of laughter, I guess. I honestly didn't think it was that funny.

"That doesn't sound very funny to me."

"Westwater. We live on West Eighty-eighth Street, right by the river."

I shrugged. "I think it's a nice name," I said as we started across the street.

"You do?" he asked in this sort of adoring voice.

Now I'd really done it. "Well, I've got to go. See you around, Michael Oliver."

"I see you made a new friend," Richard, the doorman, said to me.

"Not exactly," I said with a warning look. Richard is the worst gossip on the block.

As I went around the corner and stood waiting for the elevator, I could hear the two of them talking.

"What's her name?"

"That's Miranda Bartlett," Richard said. "She's been in the building since she was a baby."

Shut up, Richard.

"Thanks a lot," said Michael Oliver. I could just imagine him scuttling next door to write it all down in that little notebook.

4 · Feeling Left Out

When I got home, I went right into my room and sat down on my bed and thought about things. I mean what a completely strange day I was having. But one thing was bugging me more than any other. Had Phoebe gone out running with some boy? If Michael Oliver was right, that meant she had lied to me about doing homework all day. I must admit, that story had sounded fishy from the beginning.

Frisbee pushed her way through the door and put her head in my lap.

"Where have you been?" I asked as I rubbed her head. "Everybody's deserted me today just when I needed them most."

"She was with me," Alex said, sticking his head around the door. "Peter and I were in Central Park."

"Thanks for taking her out," I said. "I always feel guilty when I have to leave her inside all day Sunday.

And don't give me any lectures, Alex Bartlett. If I want to feel guilty about something, I'm going to feel guilty."

"Excuse me for breathing," he said, but he didn't leave.

I went on patting Frisbee's head. She was falling asleep sitting up.

"How was the Lower East Side?" Alex asked.

I shrugged. "It was fine. Grandpa bought some boots, and we went to Chinatown for lunch."

"Did he come home with you?"

"No, he took Margaret to Wall Street to show her his old office building. I didn't feel like going, so I came back." I didn't say anything about Michael Oliver. If Alex got his hooks into a weirdo like Michael Oliver, he'd really go to town. Guess that guy has enough problems without Dr. Bartlett in his life.

"Is that all?"

"What do you mean?" I asked.

"What about Margaret and Grandpa? How did they act with each other?"

I shrugged. "About the same as last night. No big deal."

"Oh." He turned to go.

"Except I began to feel like a third wheel after a while," I muttered.

He came back in and sat down beside me. "Physical displays of affection? Soulful sighs? Meaningful looks?"

"I thought you were all for leaving them alone. Hands-off policy," I said.

"Just doing a little research. All in the line of business."

I grinned. "Under the heading: Is it possible to fall in love over the age of sixty?"

"Well, what was it?" asked Alex.

"Meaningful looks. Long silences."

He stood up. "Not enough to go on. Keep on it, Miss Bartlett. I'll want a full report in the morning."

"Ms. Bartlett, if you please." I'm not that big a feminist, but a brother like Alex would make you run out and join all sorts of causes.

I sat and stared out the window for a while and then, in despair, started my homework. I wasn't going to call Phoebe. She could call me first.

"Miranda, hold the bus," I heard her yelling from half a block away.

"Could you wait, please? My friend's coming," I said to the driver as I showed him my pass.

"Sure," he said with a smile. What a shock. I hadn't seen him before. He must be new on the route.

"You look grim this morning," Phoebe said as she flopped down beside me. "Thanks for getting him to wait."

"It's a new driver. He actually smiled at me. I was wondering how many crabby people it would take to sour him."

Phoebe grinned. "You make the poor man sound like a pickle. You're too cynical for your tender age, Miranda."

I nodded. She was right. When you grow up in the city, you can't stay innocent too long. Just the other night, I heard my parents talking about the suburbs again. None of us wants to go, but if we moved somewhere like Bronxville, Alex and I could go to public school and Pops could get some tax breaks. Bronxville. Yuk. I didn't want to think about it.

Phoebe was buried in math homework.

"I thought you had to stay in yesterday to do your homework," I said.

She looked up. "What?" she said blankly.

"Good liars have to have good memories," I said, quoting my father. I got out a book and pretended to be reading it.

"Oh that," she said nervously. At least she sounded nervous to me. "My parents let me off the hook when they saw what a nice day it was. I called you, but there was no answer."

"Oh," I said coolly. "Too bad. I could have used the company."

We went the rest of the way in silence. "See you this afternoon," she called as we parted at the bus stop. I didn't answer.

I thought about Phoebe's lie all day long at school. By lunch, I'd decided she could have been telling the truth. I mean here I was believing some weirdo I met in the park over my best friend. Michael Oliver probably got Phoebe mixed up with someone else. By French class, I was worried she'd never speak to me again. By the time I got on the bus, I was miserable. I'm not a person who makes friends easily. Here I'd gone and thrown away the best friend I'd ever had.

I went to the phone and called her the minute I got in the front door. Her mother answered the phone.

"Is Phoebe there, Mrs. Livingston?"

"Hello, Miranda. She's just coming across to see you. You two shouldn't bother with phones. You can just communicate by telepathy."

"Good-bye. Thanks."

I hung up just as the front doorbell rang. When I opened it, we both started talking at once.

"I'm sorry I was so mean on the bus—"

"I'm sorry I lied to you about yesterday—"

Then we both stopped.

"So it was a lie," I said.

She nodded. "I'm sorry. I just wasn't sure I could trust anybody, not even you."

"What are you talking about?"

"I'm in love."

I almost fell through the floor. Suddenly everybody was falling in love. Dropping like flies all around me. "Not you too," I cried.

She nodded again solemnly. "You'd better come in," I said. "I have to be sitting down when I hear this story."

We went to my room and shut the door.

"Is Alex home yet?"

"No, but I can't promise you he hasn't bugged the room. Want to check for wires?"

"Are you kidding?" she asked. We both know how far Alex can go when he puts his mind to it.

"Yes, I'm kidding. Now, what are you talking about?"

"Remember that guy I met one day when we were jogging? He wanted to know where I got my shoes?"

I nodded.

"Well, I ran into him on Broadway Saturday, and he asked me to go running with him in the park Sunday afternoon."

So Michael Oliver was right. He had seen Phoebe. One point for Westwater.

"He's wonderful, Miranda."

I cut her off. I just didn't think I could take any gushing.

"What's his name? Where does he live?"

"His name is Philip Hightower. He lives on Eighty-third and Riverside. In that fancy co-op building."

Westwater, Hightower. What was this? "Next you're going to tell me he lives in the penthouse."

"Nope. I think he said the tenth floor. Why?"

I shrugged. "Just a joke. Hightower. Get it?"

She frowned. "I don't think you're being very serious about this, Miranda."

"Well, what do you expect me to say? My best

friend abandons me to run with some perfect stranger she's picked up in the park, then lies to me, then expects me to be happy about it. What would you do?"

She didn't answer but sat and scratched the top of Frisbee's head absentmindedly.

"Where's Dungeon?" I asked to change the subject.

"I was in such a rush to come over and tell you all this that I forgot him. I'll take him out later."

Now I started to feel bad again. I mean, at least she'd come over to tell me. When I fall in love (which I plan never to do), I guess I wouldn't want my best friend to act grumpy about it.

"Well, so tell me. What's he like?"

"He has brown eyes and blond hair," she said. "And he runs about four times a week. He's thinking of training for the Marathon next year. He wants me to go watch the one in Central Park next weekend."

Now you see. There's another thing I just assumed Phoebe and I would do together.

I guess she saw the look on my face because she said, "You could come too. I know you'd like him, Miranda."

"No thanks." No third-wheel trip for me again. "How old is he?"

"He's about sixteen, I think." She was trying to be nonchalant.

"What do your parents think about him?"

Phoebe's face fell. "That's the trouble. I don't dare tell them. I'm sure they'd lock me up and never let me out to run. You know my parents."

"Why don't you ask them? I mean, don't say, 'I want to go out with this boy.' Say, 'What do you think about girls my age going out with . . .'" My voice dribbled off. The whole sentence did sound sort of stupid.

"Last week, I was telling them about Amy, that girl in my class who's allowed to 'date' as my mother calls it, and they hit the roof. Dad went into some long lecture about parents who don't care what their children do and the evils of the city and so on."

My mind had wandered. I was trying to decide whether my parents would let me go out with some boy they didn't know.

"So I'm just going to see him on the sly. You know, when we're out running or something." She shrugged. "I don't even know why we're talking this way. He'll probably decide he can't stand me and that will be that." But I knew she didn't really believe it.

"And where do I fit in to all this?" I muttered.

"What do you mean?"

"You're running with him and going to the Marathon with him. Does he go to school on the East Side? You'll probably be taking the bus with him in the mornings."

"That's not true, Miranda. You're my best friend,

after all. Besides, he doesn't run every afternoon."

I jumped up. This conversation was getting me down. "Go get Dungeon, and I'll meet you on the corner."

"All right," she said. She seemed relieved too. "See you in five minutes."

We went down to the track. It was one of those bad days for me. My bones seemed to get in each other's way and everything ached. Phoebe doesn't ever have days like that with her body. She says she has them with her mind.

To top it off, on the way home, I saw Michael Oliver walking down the Promenade toward us. He had his pad out, and he hadn't seen us yet.

"Let's go up the hill to Eighty-third," I said quickly.

Phoebe shook her head. "That brings us right up to Philip's building. I don't want to bump into him this afternoon. He might think I'm chasing him."

She speeded up and I followed her, keeping my head down. By that time, Michael Oliver had seen us. But the most amazing thing happened. He didn't yell or run up to me or anything. As I went by, he just nodded and kept on walking. Phoebe didn't even notice.

I can't figure out that kid at all.

5 · Michael Oliver's Big News

"How did Grandpa seem when he went home?" I asked at the dinner table that night.

"Fine," Mother said. "I hear you had a great trip to the Lower East Side."

"It was fun. Margaret showed us one of her favorite restaurants in Chinatown."

"Margaret must have been out to dinner about five thousand times," Alex said. "She has a favorite restaurant in every section of the city."

"I think Grandpa might ask Margaret up to Vermont for a weekend," I said slowly.

Mother and Pops smiled. "It is wonderful that two of our favorite people like each other," Mother said. "It makes me feel all silly inside."

She gave Pops this look that always makes me stare at the floor or something. All googly-eyed as Phoebe would say. I mean I'm glad they love each other, but really! I got up and started to clear the table.

"Miranda, there's a block association meeting on Thursday. Let's go together," Pops said. "It's at eight thirty."

"All right."

My father and I like to keep up with the neighborhood. Mother goes to meetings all day so she can't stand the idea of another one, and Alex is bored by them so he makes up ridiculous reasons why he can't go. I don't care. I like having Pops all to myself once in a while.

I was walking up to Broadway a couple of days later when who should materialize at my side but Michael Oliver himself. I swear the kid just appeared out of thin air.

"Hello, Miranda."

"Who gave you leave to use my name?" I asked.

"Oh, sorry," he said wistfully.

I glanced at him. This kid has been knocked around a lot in life, I thought.

"What's up? Been keeping track of things? My running time's a little off this week. Sorry to disappoint you. Body's not up to par."

"Big news," he said solemnly.

We reached Broadway. "You got any business up here?" I asked.

He shook his head.

"I've got some errands to do for my mother. Want to tag along?"

"Sure," he said. "That's fine."

"What's the news?" I asked as we plunged into the fruit market.

"Some developers want to buy the Methodist church. They're going to knock it down and put up a high-rise."

Well, I have to admit that stopped me dead in my tracks. The Methodist church is the building just north of us on the Drive. It's low, which is why we have a view up the river. Besides that, it's a beautiful little church.

"How do you know this?" I asked.

He shrugged. "I keep track of things. I've noticed a lot of activity over there recently. People going in and out. Someone was standing out front making a sketch, and then the other day, a surveyor with one of those little telescopes was standing across the street."

"Excuse me, miss, are you in line?"

"No, not yet," I said, stepping out of the way. "Go on."

"So one day, I just hung out in the church all day. I pretended to be doing a sketch of the building for an art class. Some old lady came by and started talking to me. It turned out she had been going to the church for thirty years. When she looked at my drawing, she said it was a good thing I was sketching it up now because soon the building was going to be torn down."

I stood there staring at his funny little face in the middle of the fruit market. What an incredible detective this kid was.

"Miranda?" he said timidly. "What do you need to get in here? We're sort of in the way."

"Oh, right, grab me a bunch of those red grapes, and I'll get the salad stuff. Oh, yes, and four potatoes. The kind that you bake. Long and skinny."

We gathered everything together, and I paid for it.

"But how do you know for sure they're going to put up a high-rise?" I asked as we were walking down Broadway. "Maybe they just want to build another church."

"They don't have any money. This lady told me they're sitting on a gold mine because a piece of land on the Upper West Side is worth so much money these days."

"But where is the church going to move?"

He shrugged. "I don't know."

"Michael Oliver, we can't let this happen. This is horrible. If they put an apartment building in there, we won't have any view north up the river. I'll wake up every morning and look at somebody else brushing their teeth." I felt this horrible sense of panic coming over me.

"What about me? Our apartment doesn't even

have a view. Light and a piece of the sky is all we've got. Now even that will be gone."

"We're not going to let this happen. We're going to do something," I said firmly.

"What?"

Good question. I didn't answer it for a long time.

"I know. Tonight you're coming with me and my father to the block association meeting. We're got to organize the community." To tell the truth, I didn't know what I was talking about, but it sounded good. Michael Oliver looked hesitant. "It's at eight thirty. Will your mother let you come out then? I know it's dark, but we'll pick you up and walk you home."

"Oh, that's not the problem. She couldn't care less where I am. But I don't want to say all this stuff in front of a lot of people. You know the whole story now. Why don't you tell them what I said?"

Well, to be honest, I wasn't going to stand up and say anything in front of a big group either. But I knew Pops would do it if he believed Michael Oliver's story.

"I'll tell you what. You meet us in the lobby of our building at eight o'clock. You can tell my father just what you told me and if you can convince him, then he'll do the talking at the meeting."

Michael Oliver agreed. I said good-bye and was in our elevator before I realized I'd forgotten the other two errands.

Mother agreed to have dinner early so Pops and I could meet Michael Oliver in the lobby at eight. I refused to tell any of them anything about my "mystery guest" as Alex called him. In fact, I was nervous he'd follow us downstairs, but Mother made him do the dishes. All I needed was Alex giving me grief about hanging around with some ten year old.

Michael Oliver was waiting for us. He slid out of one of the dark corners of the lobby before we even saw him.

"You could have sat on the bench, you know," I said. "That's what they're here for."

He just shrugged. I think he likes all the sneaking around. It seems to fit his personality.

"This is my father, Mr. Bartlett. Pops, this is Michael Oliver Westwater."

"Hello, Michael Oliver," my father said, and they shook hands rather solemnly.

"Let's take a walk around the block," I said. I was still nervous that Alex might decide to come. "Michael Oliver can tell you what he's discovered."

Pops seemed a little amazed at all the mystery, but he went along with it without saying anything.

As soon as we were around the corner, Michael Oliver launched into his story. My father listened and didn't say anything until he was through. Then Pops asked him some questions. By that time, we'd gone around two blocks, and it was almost eight thirty.

"What do you think, Pops?"

"It certainly sounds possible. It would be easy to find out whether they've actually sold the building or not. It would be in the city records."

"Don't you think we should bring it up at the meeting?" I asked.

"Yes, I do. As long as we point out that it's all rumor, and we don't have any definite word on it yet."

"Michael Oliver doesn't want to say anything," I said to Pops. Even in the dark, I could feel his grateful eyes on me.

"I'll do the talking," said Pops. "But you may have to answer questions."

"You can handle that, can't you?" I said.

"I guess so," he said in this tiny voice. Michael Oliver was definitely a behind-the-scenes man.

"All right, partners, let's go," Pops said.

The meeting was just beginning when we arrived. We took some seats in the back. It was quite a big group this evening because the garbage collection schedule was on the agenda. Nothing like garbage to get people stirred up. That discussion went on for what seemed like hours. Finally, Mr. Weiss, the president, asked if there were any other matters to be discussed, and Pops stood up.

You could have heard a pin drop for about thirty seconds after he finished talking. Then everybody started asking questions at once.

"Have they actually sold the building?"

"How do you know all this?"

"Who's the developer?"

"Where is the church going?"

"Why didn't they consult with us about it?"

Mr. Weiss pounded the table with his fist and everybody quieted down so Pops could answer the questions.

"We don't know anything for sure, but I have a young man here who got this information just by being observant."

Naturally, everybody turned around and stared at Michael Oliver, and he looked as if he wanted to do one of his disappearing acts. I felt sorry for him.

"But he's just a kid," someone said, and the whole place began to get noisy again.

Anyway, after some discussion, Mr. Weiss appointed a committee to find out the situation and report to him in five days if there was anything to back up the rumors. Pops was chairman of the committee. Then the meeting was adjourned.

"Want to go up to Baskin-Robbins with us?" I asked Michael Oliver. "Pops and I always have ice cream after these meetings."

He shook his head. "No, thanks. See you." He was gone before either of us could say anything else.

"He's a funny kid," Pops said as we started up the street toward Broadway. "How did you meet him?"

"Another one of my pickups in the park," I said with a grin. "I seem to attract all the loonies."

Pops looked stern. "That's not a joking matter, Miranda. I'm going to have to put a stop to your running if you're talking to a lot of strangers."

"Come on, Pops, I'm kidding. So far I've picked one marathon maniac and one scrawny kid who thinks he's a private eye. Nothing very harmful."

"I wonder what his home life is like. I'm surprised his parents allow him to come and go at any hour of the night," Pops said.

"That makes me wonder too." We walked on in silence for a little while. "Listen, Pops, Michael Oliver is my secret, okay? I don't want Phoebe or Alex to know about him."

He smiled. "It's a deal." He pulled open the door to Baskin-Robbins. "Right this way, madame," he said with a sweeping bow. "Your usual table?"

My father acts like a nut sometimes, but that's why I like him.

6 · Phoebe Asks Me to Lie

Michael Oliver was right. My father did some calling around and checking on the records. The church hadn't sold the building yet, but they were negotiating with a developer.

"They haven't signed a contract," Pops explained. "But they admit they are close to it."

"How high will the building go?" Mother asked.

"I talked to a friend up the street, Dan Jordan. He's an architect who knows the city zoning rules. He says they can go up thirty stories."

"Oh no," Mother gasped. We all sat in silence for a long horrible moment, thinking about it. We're on the seventh floor. A building that tall would mean we wouldn't even see the sky.

"And how close to us can they build?" Alex asked.

"I think up to their plot line, which is about fifteen feet from our north windows."

"I feel like the character in that Edgar Allan Poe story who was bricked in behind a wall. What can we do?" I asked Pops.

"I looked up a little bit of history on the church. It was built in 1879 by quite a famous architect of the period. I think we should fight to have it landmarked."

"What does that mean?" Alex asked.

"There's a commission set up in New York to designate certain buildings as landmarks. That means the exterior cannot be altered or torn down." Pops shrugged. "I'm not an architect, but I certainly think this building has a great deal of architectural merit."

"You've got to think about the people too," Mother said quietly. "Maybe there's some way we could help them raise some money so they wouldn't have to sell the church."

"I know," Pops said. "I've been thinking about that." He stood up. This discussion had taken place around the breakfast table, and we were all running late as a result. "There's going to be a meeting of our committee tonight at eight thirty. Dan, this architect, has agreed to come to it, and I thought I'd ask Margaret to join us."

"We'd better get out of here," Mother said suddenly. "Leave the dishes. We're all going to be late."

I ran into Phoebe on the bus coming home. I told her about the building. She looked as if she was trying to concentrate on what I was saying, but her mind was definitely wandering.

"You aren't listening to me," I said.

"Yes, I really am, Miranda," she said.

"Have you started carving Phoebe and Phil on the trees in the park?"

"He doesn't like to be called Phil," she said. "That's why he likes my name. No way to make a nickname out of it."

We got off the bus and started home. "There's something I want to tell you, Miranda. Last night, my parents said they wanted to come to the park and watch the Marathon with me so I told them I was going with you. I don't want them to find out about Philip." She rolled her eyes. "Part of the togetherness kick. Get interested in the things your daughter likes."

"Aw, come on, Phoebe. You've got to give them a chance. At least they're trying."

"Anyway, I told them that we were going out to lunch with your parents and that you had asked me ages ago but I'd just forgotten to tell them."

"Sounds complicated," I said. I hate to lie. I'm not very good at it.

"I know, but they'll never call and check on me as long as I'm supposed to be with you. My parents think you're the one healthy friend I have. In fact, Mother told me to ask you for dinner soon. 'We haven't seen Miranda in ages.' You can just hear her."

"I'll come anytime," I said with a grin. The food was always great over there. Only bad thing was I had to wear a skirt, but we all have to suffer sometime.

"See you. Don't forget to cover for me," she called.

"Hey, Phoebe, tell your parents about the church," I yelled across the street.

"What church?"

"Oh, never mind," I called.

"I remember. I'll tell them."

She hadn't really been listening. Just as I thought.

On the way into my building, I stopped Richard. "Have you seen that kid I was talking to the other day? The skinny one with glasses?"

Richard shook his head. "Not in a couple of days."

"Well, if you see him go by, can you get him to call me on the intercom? There's something I want to talk to him about."

"Oh, so you did make friends with him?" Richard asked. He really is the living end, as my mother would say. "That's nice. He's a lonely kid. I never see him hanging around with anybody else."

"See you, Richard," I said in my cool voice as I stepped into the elevator.

I changed into jeans and sat down at my desk. I didn't want to run. It was really cold out and the cold weather sometimes brings on my asthma. Frisbee whined and pushed her head onto my lap.

"I'll take you out later, girl."

I heard Alex come in, but I didn't say anything to him. I was struggling with a math problem, which actually meant I was looking out the window a lot. The trouble is every time I looked out the window, I thought about the church being torn down. I began to daydream about being some character from outer space throwing an impenetrable shield around the building when Alex called to me.

"Miranda, come here a minute."

"Why?"

"You wouldn't believe this guy. I want you to look at him."

"I'm not going to snoop on some poor, unsuspecting soul just because you choose to." But I got up anyway. The math problem was not getting solved.

"Here, take the binoculars. You can almost see what he's writing."

Well, you know I had this eerie feeling even before I stepped to the window. Alex pointed out the figure, and I looked down through the binoculars at . . . Michael Oliver Westwater! I stood there for a long time, pretending to study him. Suddenly, Michael Oliver snapped his pad shut and went back in through the window. I was glad he went inside just then. I don't think I could have stood watching him one more minute.

"He's gone," I said, handing the binoculars back to Alex.

"Could you see what he wrote down?"

I shook my head and started back into my room. I didn't want to give away anything.

"I'm not sure what I'm going to do when it gets too cold for him to come out on the fire escape. I can watch the living room and the kitchen from here, but all I can see is his mother."

"What does she look like?" I asked, trying to sound nonchalant. At least Michael Oliver had a mother. I was beginning to think he lived alone.

"Kind of wacky. She walks around with curlers in her hair. I don't know anybody who does that anymore." Alex started writing something on a piece of paper.

"What are you doing?"

"Making notes on what I saw today."

"From the sound of it, you and this fellow would really like each other. You both use binoculars and notepads."

Alex's fist came smashing down on the desk.

"That's it, Miranda. I bet he knows something about the church. That's why he sits over there and watches it all the time."

"Maybe," I said as I slipped out the door. This whole conversation was getting too close for comfort. "I've got to take Frisbee out."

We took a brisk walk through the park. It was a beautiful fall day with the trees turning red and gold and the sky a purple blue.

I couldn't decide what I was going to do about Alex

and Michael Oliver. Knowing Alex, I was sure if I told him I knew Michael Oliver, he would start bugging me to invite the poor guy over. He might even start following me around. After thinking about it for a long time, I decided not to say anything, at least for now. Maybe Alex would give up the whole project after a while.

On the way home, we passed the church. On an impulse, I tied Frisbee to the fence and tiptoed inside.

It was dark and still, the way churches always are, especially in the city. A silent shadowy place in the middle of the noise and light of New York. I sat down in the back and looked carefully around. It was a simple church, which made me like it. There were arches in the ceiling and over the altar as well as down both sides above the stained glass windows. It felt peaceful just sitting there until someone slid into the pew beside me. It was Michael Oliver. I might have known.

"How did you know I was here?" I asked.

"I saw Frisbee tied up outside. She doesn't look very happy."

"I know. She hates being tied up. I had a sudden inspiration to look at this place on the way home."

We sat there a minute longer and then I motioned to him. "Come outside. I have news for you."

We walked around the block a couple of times

while I told him what Pops had found out. He seemed sort of stunned.

"I really was right then?" he said. "I was beginning to think I was imagining the whole thing. What happens next?"

I told him about the commission that saves buildings. "Pops said it's going to be very hard to stop."

We turned and looked back at the church. "I like the stained glass windows the most," he said slowly. "I've been copying their designs in my pad." He flipped it to the right page and held it out to me. "No saints or halos or anything. Just flowers and different kinds of curlicues. I guess they're supposed to make you think of God without sticking him right in front of your face."

"You're a good artist," I said as I handed him back his precious pad.

He shrugged. "I'm good at copying things."

"Where do you go to school?"

He didn't answer for a long time. "Public School 166," he muttered.

"What do you think of it?"

"I don't pay much attention to it. As long as everybody leaves me alone, I'm just fine."

I was going to ask him about his family, but I could see him sort of shrinking away from me. He obviously didn't like talking about himself.

When we got back to my building, I stopped him as he was turning away.

"What's your phone number?"

"We don't have a phone. My mother forgot to pay the bill, so they took it out a couple of months ago."

"How do I find you if I need to tell you something?" I asked.

"Don't worry, I'll check in with you," he said as he turned away.

His skinny back in that blue jeans jacket made me feel sad.

" 'Bye," I called, but he didn't answer.

7 · In the Middle

The meeting that night was interesting. I sat on the side and took notes so I could tell Michael Oliver about it. The architect told us how to get the Landmarks Preservation Commission to set a hearing date.

"The commission makes a decision on whether to designate a building or not purely on architectural merit," he said. "If we really want to do this the right way, I think we should hire an architectural historian to do a report on the church."

"How much will that cost?" Pops asked.

"Well, if we get a graduate student, about five hundred dollars."

"Where are we going to get that kind of money?" Mother asked.

"Wait a minute," Margaret said. "I think we're getting a little ahead of ourselves here. The first thing we should do is talk to the minister and the administrative board of the church. Let's hear their reasons for selling. Maybe there's a way we could help them raise some money so they could stay there."

"That's an excellent idea, Margaret," Pops said. "I'll set up a time for the two of us to do that. Meanwhile, Dan, you could look around for somebody to do this research, and we'll meet again next Monday."

They all agreed to that plan. Margaret signaled to me as she was headed out the door. "Want to come help me finish up a cake?" she said. I hesitated. I still had my homework to do. "It's raspberry nut," she said.

"Let's go," I said. Raspberry nut cake is my absolute favorite.

We settled ourselves down in her living room and munched away in silence for a while. I had a feeling Margaret had something on her mind. I hadn't seen her at all since our trip to the Lower East Side, and I think she knew I'd been avoiding her.

"Did Grandpa show you his office?" I asked. "That day after I left you?"

She looked a little blank. "I suppose he did. It seems to me we walked all over the place. He does have an incredible amount of energy, your grandfather. He proposed we walk home from the Village, but I said no to that. I assume you got home all right on the subway. With his worrying, I began to feel a little guilty about letting you go off alone. You should have stayed with us."

I shrugged. "I came back and went running. That was the day I met Michael Oliver in the park. He's the one who told us about the church."

"Your father mentioned that the information had come through you but he couldn't divulge the source. It all sounded very mysterious. Who is Michael Oliver?"

I told her as much as I knew about him. "He's a funny sad sort of kid. I think I'm the first person he's ever been friends with."

"He's lucky to have you," she said slowly. There was a little silence. I got up and took our plates to the sink.

"Your grandfather has invited me up for a weekend in Vermont," she said.

I didn't say anything.

"How do you feel about me going, Miranda?"

"Why does that make any difference?" I asked. I was trying to sound casual but it came out sounding rude.

She came up and put her arm around my shoulders. "It makes a difference because we both love you very much, and we don't want you to feel left out of something."

I just knew if I stood there one more minute, I was going to cry. Now isn't that the dumbest thing you've ever heard of? "I've got to run, Margaret. I've got tons of homework, and I haven't even started. I'll talk to you later, okay?" I babbled my way out of the apartment. Thank heavens, the elevator came right away, or she might have followed me into the hall. How could I tell her how I felt about something when I just wasn't sure?

"Phoebe called, Miranda," my mother said as I went zooming past the kitchen door. "She wants you to call her right back."

"Okay," I mumbled and went into my room to pull myself together.

When I finally got around to calling Phoebe, she answered the phone.

"Listen, Mother is cooking up some plan for us all to go to lunch together before the Marathon. I told her I didn't think we could horn in on your plans, so then she complained she never sees you anymore. Could you please come for dinner tomorrow night? I know it's a drag, Miranda, but then she'll stop bugging me, and I can go with 'you know who' to the Marathon." Her voice had dropped to a whisper, and I could barely hear her.

"Isn't there some line about tangled webs and lying?" I asked. "Is this guy really worth all this?"

"Please, Phoebe, he's the first person who's ever asked me out. Please help me." She sounded so desperate that I couldn't refuse. I wondered if I'd ever feel this way about a boy.

"You're on. Let me just ask Mother." I put my

hand over the receiver. "Can I go to the Livingstons' for dinner tomorrow night?" Mother nodded. "It's fine. What time?"

"I'm not sure. I'll tell you tomorrow on the bus. Thanks, Miranda."

I was about to hang up when I heard her talking again.

"Don't forget that we're going to the Marathon together, in case she brings it up."

"I won't forget," I said.

"Big crisis?" Mother asked as I headed back into my room.

"Not really," I said. "You know how dramatic Phoebe can be over little things."

I got my homework done in record time that night, mainly because I didn't want to think about Margaret and Grandpa, and I didn't want to think about Alex watching Michael Oliver, and I didn't want to think about lying for Phoebe. My life has never been so complicated, and I don't like it.

Dinner went off just fine. Phoebe's parents like me because I'm sort of normal and polite, and I definitely appreciate their food. My mother's a good cook, but she doesn't have time to do anything exciting in the kitchen. Alex is the "inspirational" cook in our house, but nobody would want to eat what he comes up with. Phoebe's parents are very rich and when you go there for dinner, you get served by a maid, and her parents drink wine out of crystal glasses. Maybe you'd get sick of that routine if you had to go through it every night. That must be why Phoebe likes to come to my house.

"Miranda, I think it's wonderful that you're all going to watch the Marathon together," said Mrs. Livingston. "I didn't know that your parents were so interested in running."

I could feel Phoebe giving me the eyeball. "It's just since I've been running," I said. "But my brother Alex has always been very involved in exercise."

"That's putting it mildly," Phoebe said. "He's what you might call a health nut. He won't even let us have an ice cream cone in front of him."

I knew she was trying to get her mother off the Marathon thing, but Mrs. Livingston would not give up.

"Now, where will you sit to watch it? I hear it gets very crowded around the finish line."

"Last year, we went up by the Museum. There are some nice rocks there you can sit on. We took a picnic. It was very warm." I was getting pretty good at this lying stuff.

"Were you running last year, Miranda?" asked Mr. Livingston. "I thought Phoebe was the one who started you on that in the spring."

Uh-oh, guess I wasn't very good at it. "That's right,

but last year Alex dragged us out." Short silence. Everybody fiddled with their forks. I was madly trying to think of something to say.

"Have you heard about the Methodist church?" I asked. Everybody looked at me blankly.

"What, dear?" said Mrs. Livingston.

"The Methodist church that's just north of our building. They're talking about selling out to a developer who wants to put up a high-rise. My father says they could go as high as thirty stories."

"It would ruin the view from Miranda's window. She'd have to watch people eating breakfast instead of the boats going up the river," Phoebe said.

"But it's not just that," I said. "The other day I actually went into the church. It's really pretty. There's a nice stained-glass window right above the altar with beautiful flowers in it. It made me sad to think they might knock down something like that just to put up another apartment building."

"That's progress for you," said Mr. Livingston, pushing his chair back from the table. "I'm rather pleased to hear it, frankly. It shows what a good investment the West Side has become."

"But, Daddy, all you ever think about is the investment. The Methodist church is a beautiful building that was built years and years ago."

"They don't build like that anymore, dear," said Mrs. Livingston in a little voice. I think she is scared of her husband.

"We don't want this neighborhood to look like the East Side," I said in a horrified voice. That's what I'd heard someone say last night at the meeting. "Those buildings over on York Avenue look like jails instead of places to live."

He smiled at me in this condescending way. "It's a very complicated question, Miranda."

"Let's go into the other room," said Mrs. Livingston. "We'll have our coffee in there, Bridget."

Well, by that time, I was getting pretty mad. I didn't want to sit in the other room and make small talk. Phoebe rescued us.

"I've got a lot of homework, Mother. Miranda brought her books over so we could do it together."

"We wouldn't want to keep you girls from that," Mr. Livingston said. "Go right ahead."

"I guess I was sort of rude to your father," I said to Phoebe when we were back in her room.

She shrugged. "He's a real pain to argue with. He always ends up by saying you don't know as much as he does. You never get anywhere with him."

We didn't get much work done because Phoebe kept interrupting to tell me about Philip. I went home early and finished it there.

8 · Alex Meets His Subject

I ended up going to the Marathon after all. With Michael Oliver.

He was coming out of his building when I was walking over to Central Park with Frisbee.

"Hi," he said in that shy voice.

"Hi, where are you going?"

He shrugged. "Nowhere special. How about you?"

"I'm walking over to watch the Marathon. Want to come? You could get a lot of material for your notebook."

"You don't mind?"

"Michael Oliver, you've got to get a more positive attitude about yourself. Now, why should I mind? You always look like you expect me to punch you in the face or something. Would I ask you to come if I didn't want you to?"

"I guess not," he said.

I didn't mean to go ranting on but I didn't apologize. Everything I said was true.

"Any word on the church?" he asked.

"My father and some other people went over and talked to the minister and several members of the congregation to try and convince them not to sell. Apparently, they've run out of money and plan to share space with another church on Amsterdam Avenue, so selling the building seems like the best solution to them. Pops told them that the block association was going to ask the commission to hold a public hearing on the building to see if it could be landmarked. I guess they weren't too happy about that because it would stop the sale and they'd be left with a church that they can't even afford to heat."

"Maybe there's another Methodist church that would come and share this one," Michael Oliver said.

"That's a good idea," I said, glancing at him. This kid was pretty smart. "I'll tell Pops. What've you been doing?"

"Nothing much. School's driving me crazy, my mother's driving me crazy. What else is new?"

"How about your father? Does he drive you crazy?"

"My father moved to California when I was six," he said. "I haven't seen him since then."

"Oh gosh, Michael Oliver, I'm sorry, I didn't know that."

He shrugged. "Who cares? He was a creep anyhow. My mother changed her name back, but I'm still stuck with Westwater."

"Westwater is a very nice name, Michael Oliver. At least, it's a lot more interesting than Bartlett." I was saying that to cheer him up, but I don't think it worked. He still looked glum. We walked the rest of the way in silence.

The park was pretty crowded when we got there, so we headed north along the drive until the crowds began to thin out.

"It's really hot for October," I said. "It's going to be a tough race."

"Here's a good place," said Michael Oliver, pointing to some rocks. We climbed to the top and settled ourselves down. I'd brought along the section from the newspaper that listed the runners. I showed it to Michael Oliver and pointed out the people we should watch for. Every so often three or four police cars would come screaming down the drive, their loudspeakers yelling at everybody to get out of the way, the runners were coming. We stood up on the rocks so we could see better. Down the road we could hear the crowd cheering. Then the first guy came into view. The sweat was pouring off him but he wasn't hurting at all. Just cruising along, his legs going up and down as if they were part of a machine. The second runner was only about a minute behind him, with a man breathing down his neck. I was cheering like mad. Michael Oliver had his notebook out and was scribbling things down.

"First woman," I yelled in his ear. "Write that down, Michael Oliver. Number 56. Way to go," I cheered, completely caught up in all the enthusiasm.

After about twenty minutes, the runners began to come in a pack, hundreds and hundreds of them. The longer we stayed and watched, the worse everybody began to look. But the crowd just kept cheering them on, calling out their numbers.

"Way to go, 482. Just three more miles. Shade just down the hill. Keep it up, Atlanta. Looking good."

It made me want to cry, watching those people who had trained for so many weeks, putting their all into this thing. They'd been running in the heat for almost four hours. It seemed unbelievable.

"How many are in this race?" Michael Oliver asked.

"Fourteen thousand registered to run. They say about ten thousand will finish. Ten thousand people," I yelled. "Can you imagine ten thousand people running twenty-six miles?"

Michael Oliver didn't answer. He just put the facts into his notebook.

We left after about two hours and walked slowly home. I didn't say anything. I was still feeling very moved by the whole experience, but I didn't think Michael Oliver felt the same way. As long as everything was written down in his notebook, he didn't have to think about it. Maybe it was his way of avoiding feeling things.

I was turning this over in my mind when he spoke. "Can I come up to your place?" he asked. "Nobody's home at my house."

"Sure," I said without really thinking. It wasn't until we were in the elevator that I remembered Alex. What if Alex saw Michael Oliver? The person he's been watching through binoculars this whole time sitting in his very own living room. But now I was stuck. I couldn't go back down. Alex had said something about going over to Peter's. I just prayed he had stuck to his plans.

I opened the front door very slowly and listened. Silence. "Anybody home?" I called. Still no answer. Phew.

"Well, I guess everybody's out," I said, as I led Michael Oliver into the kitchen. I took off Frisbee's leash and she lay down on the living room rug. "Want some orange juice? We don't have much else. My brother's a health food nut, so we're not allowed to have Coke or anything poisonous in the house."

"I didn't know you had a brother," he said.

"Unfortunately, I do." Oh, if only you knew what kind of a brother.

But he wasn't listening. He'd seen the river. He settled down in a chair without saying anything. I was used to this. Most people act this way when they first come in our apartment. The trouble was I couldn't afford to have Michael Oliver sitting around here all day. I had no idea when Alex would come in.

"It's really a beautiful river, isn't it?" he said, as I put the orange juice down in front of him. "The East River is just a stream compared to the Hudson."

"That's right," I said. "Here's your juice."

But he didn't pick it up. "Look, there's a tanker coming," he said. "It's just behind the Monument." He picked up the binoculars we always keep by the window and watched it steam by.

"The people look like ants running around on deck."

"You know, Michael Oliver, I'm afraid we have to go. I completely forgot an errand I was supposed to do for my mother." His face fell. "I'm really sorry, but you can come back another time. Here, I'll just get your coat while you drink your juice."

"Could I just look out the north windows?" he asked. "I'd like to see what the bridge looks like from here."

"Uh, okay. But we'd better hurry."

We were standing there, looking down at the church, when I heard the front door close. My heart dropped. I could tell by the footsteps that it was Alex.

"Miranda?"

I didn't answer for a minute.

"Who's that?" Michael Oliver asked.

"My brother," I said in a whisper.

"Miranda, are you home?" His head poked in my bedroom door. "Hi." I was watching Alex's face as Michael Oliver turned around. It was a study.

"Hi," said Michael Oliver.

"This is my brother, Alex," I mumbled. "Alex, this is Michael Oliver."

For once, my brother was stunned into silence. Michael Oliver, on the other hand, seemed quite chatty.

"This is the first time I've seen the river from this high up. Miranda was just showing me the north view. You guys are really lucky to live here."

"I know," said Alex. "It's great. Uh, where do you live?"

As if he didn't know.

"I live right next door. You can probably even see my window from here."

He walked into Alex's room with the two of us following him. This was like some horrible nightmare.

"Well, you can see the fire escape that goes next to my room. I'm surprised you haven't noticed me. I like to sit out there a lot."

"Really?" Alex said in a squeaky little voice that didn't sound like him at all.

"Sure. That's how I figured out all that stuff about the church. I'm the one who told Miranda they were going to knock it down. Didn't she tell you?"

He looked at the two of us.

"No," Alex said. "Miranda keeps a lot of things from me." The look he was giving me was withering. "Would you excuse us a minute, Michael Oliver? There's something I'd like to talk to my sister about."

Alex grabbed my arm and dragged me out into the living room. "How long have you known him?"

"I refuse to answer that question on the grounds that it—"

"Miranda, sometimes you drive me bats. But never mind. This is closer to Michael Oliver than I ever would have gotten by myself. I was just about ready to give him up and write a paper on you. So if you just keep him talking and keep him coming over, I'll go back to my original plan. Got it?" he said, and he squeezed my upper arm so hard that I screamed.

Michael Oliver appeared around the corner. "I've got to go home now," he said, looking at the two of us.

"Do you have to go so soon? I was going to have a drink of something. Don't you want to stay?" Alex said, bustling into the kitchen.

"He's just had some orange juice," I said.

Michael Oliver was hesitating.

"I'll go down in the elevator with you," I said.

Alex glared at me, but it did no good. Michael Oliver was heading for the front door.

"Listen, you come back any time you want to look at the river," Alex said. "Seriously, we have people drop by all the time."

"Really? You wouldn't mind?"

"Not at all. We'd love it. You could even come for dinner some time."

I hooked the leash on Frisbee and went to buzz for the elevator. "Come on, Michael Oliver," I said when the elevator door opened. If we waited much longer, Alex would be inviting him to move in with us.

"Your brother's very nice," Michael Oliver said as we went down.

I didn't answer. I didn't know where to start trying to explain Alex to poor innocent Michael Oliver.

9 · My First Date

Phoebe came over the next day. Alex was home, so we closeted ourselves in my bedroom.

"How was it?" I asked.

"Wonderful," she said with this starry look in her eyes. "He brought a picnic and we sat up on this hill above the Museum where we had a really good view. It's great to watch something like the Marathon with someone who cares about it as much as you do."

I nodded, remembering how irritated I'd felt with Michael Oliver and his notebook. "It was amazing, wasn't it? Ten thousand people running twenty-six miles. Kind of restores your faith in mankind."

"We felt that way too. All those people on the sidelines cheering them on. Anyway, then we went for a long walk through the park and had some cupcakes at that little café by the boat pond. It was kind of romantic."

I fixed her with a beady eye. "Did anything happen?"

"No, not that. But I think he likes me. He wants me to go to the movies with him next weekend. He has a friend, and he wants you to go too. I've told him about you."

"Me? Are you kidding? Forget it. No way."

"Come on, Miranda. You can't avoid boys forever, and I'd be there too. The guy's name is Eric Ferris."

I rolled my eyes. "I don't even like his name. Besides, I'm sure my parents would say no. What are you going to tell your parents this time?"

She shifted around on the bed. "I was going to tell them I was spending the night with you."

"You can't go on like this forever, Phoebe. They're going to find out eventually. If Philip's so nice, they'd probably let you go out with him anyway."

"My parents? Are you kidding?"

I must admit I didn't see much hope on that score. The trouble with Phoebe's parents is they don't trust her at all. But then I thought, why should they? It was kind of a vicious circle.

"Listen, Miranda, I really want you to come with us. I've never been out with Philip at night and I'm kind of nervous about what we'd say to each other. It would be so much easier if you were around. Philip says this guy Eric is very nice. We'd just go up to the New Yorker Theater and come back again. If you want, we could meet them on the corner. You wouldn't even have to tell your parents we were going out with two boys."

I shook my head. "I'm not going to lie to them. I couldn't anyway. My father'd be able to tell in a minute. If they say I can go, then I will."

They said yes, but they wanted to meet the boys first.

"And Phoebe's parents have said yes?"

"I guess so," I said. "I haven't asked her." So there you are. I said I wasn't going to lie to my parents and I already had.

"Well, as long as it's all right with them," my mother said. "It's fine with us. But we do want you to get home right after the movie."

"Your first date," said Dr. Bartlett from the end of the table. "You are really growing up." Alex is for the birds. The only date he's ever been on is to take his friend Peter's sister to a nutrition exhibit at the Coliseum. Big deal. Imagine sitting around chewing soybean nuts with a girl.

The doorbell rang. Pops came back with Margaret.

"Hello everybody," she said with a bright smile.

"Sit down, Margaret," my mother said. "We were just going to have some coffee. Would you like some?"

"Yes, thanks. I always seem to time my visits with your meals." She hesitated. "I just got in from Vermont, and I thought you'd like to know that Kevin and I have decided to get married."

Well, for a moment, you could have heard a pin drop. Then everybody was whooping and hollering and hugging and dancing around. Pops got a bottle of wine out of the icebox, and he even gave me and Alex a glass. I hadn't said much, and I could feel Margaret watching me.

"Where are you going to live?" I asked quietly when we'd settled down a bit.

"I'm going to move to Vermont," she said. "That's the only part of it that makes me sad, but I won't sell the apartment. I think I'll just rent it for a while and see how it works out. And I'm afraid you're going to have to put up with regular visits from us. I can't believe I'm going to be leaving New York."

"Have you set the date?" Mother asked.

"Not yet. We've decided to let the whole idea sink in for a little while in case one of us changes our mind." She smiled. "It is sort of crazy, you know. Two old fogies like us hitching up."

"You make it sound like a team of horses," Pops said with a grin.

"That makes you our stepgrandmother," Alex said slowly. Now isn't that funny. I hadn't thought of that before. It suddenly made me feel a lot happier.

"If I had to go out in the world and choose a grandmother, I couldn't have picked a better one," I said raising my glass. Everybody cheered and drank some more wine, and Margaret hugged me so hard I wanted to cry. But then, I was feeling a little emotional, what with the wine and all.

"I just wish you weren't going so far away," I said. "Did you try to convince Grandpa to move to New York?"

Margaret smiled. "I admit I didn't even try, Miranda. I know how unhappy he'd be. He's in his element, tramping around in the mud up there. I'm truly amazed that he ever lived in the city at all."

"I guess so," I said.

"Don't worry. I'll come down lots of times. And you could come stay with us for a whole month in the summer if you'd like."

I nodded. That would be great, but the summer seemed far away.

"Miranda's going on her first date next Saturday night," Alex said. "She may be too busy to leave the city next summer."

I glared at Alex. After thirteen years of living with my brother, I've finally learned it's better to keep quiet than try and answer him.

"Who's the lucky man?" Margaret asked.

"Eric Ferris," I said. "I've never met him. He'll probably be a creep. I'm just doing it to keep Phoebe company."

Saturday, Phoebe came over about five o'clock. She took a bath and then started to douse herself in all these creams and perfumes she'd stolen from her mother's bureau.

"This place smells like a department store," Alex

roared through our closed door. "What's going on in there? Did you spill something?"

I put my finger up to my lips. "He's like Frisbee," I whispered to Phoebe. "If you ignore him long enough, he eventually goes away."

"Alex, leave those girls alone," I heard my father say.

Phoebe had also lugged over a suitcase with about five different outfits in it. I wondered what her mother thought about that, but I didn't ask. She tried on every single one of them and asked me what I thought as she walked up and down in front of the mirror. I sat on the bed and tried to make bright comments, but after a while I began to run out of things to say.

"Now how about this? I like the green pants with this blue shirt, but I think it looks too dressed up. What do you think?"

"It looks fine. But I like the skirt better."

"But nobody wears skirts anymore. I don't want to look old-fashioned. What if I put this vest over the blouse?"

I shrugged. "Okay."

"That's not very enthusiastic. You look as if you're about to go to sleep."

"Listen, Phoebe, you've been switching outfits for the last hour. You look like a regular Barbie doll commercial. I bet Philip isn't going to even notice what you're wearing."

"Of course he will. So what're you going to wear?"

"What I've got on," I said.

"Those old blue jeans? You're kidding." She shook her head dramatically. "This may be the most important moment of your life, and you don't even change your clothes."

"Now, listen, I'm sure Eric Ferris will be all right, but I don't think this is the most important moment of my life. Besides, I like the casual relaxed look," I said as I went out of the room.

In the end she wore her blue jeans too.

"After all that, look what they're wearing," Alex said when we appeared in the kitchen. "Blue jeans. The uniform of the hip generation. Can't you two break out of the mold, be your own people?"

"Mother," I said in a pleading voice.

"Alex, you can leave the room unless you're going to be polite. You both look fine. After all, they're just going to the movies on Broadway."

The doorbell rang. Alex answered it before I could get there.

"Good evening, may I help you?"

"Uh, yes, is Phoebe Livingston here?"

"Right this way, sir. Your name, please." Alex was putting on his butler act. I decided to go and put a stop to it before he got even more outrageous.

"Hi, I'm Miranda," I said, as I stepped out of the kitchen.

They both said hi and everybody sort of stared at

their feet. Eric Ferris was tall and gangly with blond hair. He looked even more nervous than the rest of us if that was possible. My parents came out and introduced themselves. Then I got our coats and yelled for Phoebe, who seemed to have disappeared into thin air. Finally, she came down the hall and said hello. I guess that was supposed to be the grand entrance. Too much.

The elevator ride seemed to take forever. I've noticed that elevators are about the most uncomfortable places to be with somebody else. Either you're having a private conversation and someone steps in so you have to stop talking or you're stuck with the lady from 14A who has two yapping miniature poodles who try to eat the cuffs of your pants. No way to feel comfortable in the elevator, particularly with a blind date who looks even more miserable than you do.

Of course, who should we run into smack dab in front of our building but Michael Oliver. I saw him coming and tried to make wild don't-talk-to-me-now signals with my face, but I guess he didn't see them in the dark.

"Miranda, guess what? The landmarks commission set a hearing on the Methodist church. Sometime in December. That means they can't knock it down before then."

"Great, that's great. See you around," I said, and I kept walking.

"Who was that guy?" Phoebe asked. "How do you know him?"

I shrugged. "He's working on saving the church with my father."

"He looks about ten years old," Philip said.

"Miranda has always liked younger men," Phoebe said with a smirk.

They both burst out laughing. I gave Phoebe a dirty look but she missed it. She and Philip were walking on ahead.

"What church?" asked Eric Ferris. That was the first thing he'd said all night, and I could see why. The poor guy had this strange squeaky voice that made him sound as if he had a piece of raw carrot stuck in his throat. Sort of a strangled noise.

"Excuse me?" I said.

"What church are you trying to save?"

I'd actually heard him but I wanted to test the voice. It sounded the same the second time around.

I launched into the story of the Methodist church and went on babbling all the way to the movie theater. Every time I glanced over at Eric Ferris, he actually seemed to be listening. Or maybe he was just glad he didn't have to be talking.

The movie wasn't bad, but I didn't pay much attention to it because there was a lot of squirming and giggling from Philip and Phoebe, who were sitting behind us. Eric sat like Old Stoneface, staring at the screen without moving a muscle. I guess he was embarrassed by the two of them. I kept wishing I had eyes in the back of my head so I could see what was going on.

After the movie, we went to this coffee shop and had milkshakes. Philip took out a pack of cigarettes and lit one. Then he offered a cigarette to Phoebe and she took it. My eyes almost popped out of my head. I knew she was just trying to be cool, but I couldn't let it go without saying something.

"I haven't seen you smoke before, Phoebe," I said, ignoring the dirty look she gave me. "That's not going to help your running very much." I sure did sound prim.

She shrugged. "Oh, I only do it once in a while. When I feel like it."

We took another sip of our milkshakes.

"I know this disco place up the street," Philip said. "Why don't we go dancing? They even have a bar downstairs."

I looked at Phoebe and waited for her to say no. But she didn't. By that time, I should have realized that if Philip suggested we jump off a bridge, she'd agree.

"That's a great idea," she said.

"I can't—"

"Not me—"

Eric and I both stopped and looked at each other in relief. Then I started again. "I can't," I said. "I've got to get home."

"Same here," said Eric.

"You're a couple of stick-in-the-muds," said Philip. "Come on, it'll be fun."

He just wanted us to back him up. I bet he'd never even been to that disco. The more I got to know this guy the less I liked him.

I stood up. "I really have to go," I said. "Can I talk to you for a minute, Phoebe?" We went into a huddle in the corner.

"I know what you're going to say. Your parents will want to know where I am. Just tell them I decided to spend the night at home after all. Then if you leave the door on the latch, I'll sneak in later."

"Boy, when you want to do something, you don't care what you say to cover it up, do you?"

She looked sort of shocked. "Please, Miranda, this is really important to me. You're the only one I can count on. Please do it."

I shrugged. "All right, Phoebe, but this is the last time. I'm not going to do any more lying for you."

"Thanks, Miranda, you're great." She glanced back at the boys. "I wish you'd come with us. I'm a little nervous."

"No, thanks. Eric's nice, but we don't have much to talk about. Besides . . ." I shrugged. "Never mind." I decided not to give any morality lectures.

We went back to the table, and I said good-bye. Eric stood up and said he'd walk me home, which I thought was pretty nice.

"How do you know Philip?" I asked on the way home.

"His mother and my mother are first cousins. They keep trying to get us together, but Philip and I are very different."

"I can tell," I mumbled. I was starting to get asthma so I tried to wheeze quietly, which is pretty hard to do. Please keep talking, Eric, I prayed. But he'd stopped.

At the corner of West End Avenue, I gave up trying to hide it and took a deep breath. That helped a little but the noise was pretty bad.

"Are you all right?" he asked nervously.

"Yes, it's just asthma. The smoke must have gotten to me."

"Do you get this often?"

I slowed down to catch my breath again. "Not anymore," I said. "Not since I've been running."

"Don't talk if you don't want to," he said. "Just concentrate on breathing."

I had to smile at that. The poor guy probably thought I was going to drop dead in my tracks.

We walked home slowly. "Don't come up," I said, waving him away. "I'm fine now. Thanks a lot. It was nice meeting you."

"Sure. Maybe I'll see you again sometime. 'Bye." He went away looking relieved that I was off his hands.

When I got upstairs, everybody had gone to bed.

I switched the lock on the front door and went into the kitchen to pour myself some milk. Mother came down the hall.

"Hello, dear, how was it?"

"Fine," I said. "Not very exciting."

"Where's Phoebe?"

I turned back to the icebox. I'm a terrible liar if someone can see my face. "Oh, she decided to spend the night at home after all."

"Oh, dear. Did you have a fight or something?"

"No, I think she didn't want to listen to my wheezing all night."

"Do you have your inhaler?"

"Yes, it's in my room. Good night, Mother. I think I'll go to bed now." I thought everybody'd better get to bed before Phoebe came tromping in. "Mother, don't tell Pops about the asthma, he worries too much about it."

She smiled. "All right, Miranda. I won't say a word."

The asthma comes from my father's side so he feels guilty about it. Sometimes he likes to sit up and keep me company until I can fall asleep, which is very sweet of him, but that was the last thing I needed tonight.

I crawled into bed and lay there for what seemed like hours waiting for Phoebe's footsteps down the hall. Finally, I fell asleep.

10 · I Talk to Alex

She was there in the morning. I don't know what I would have done if she hadn't been. Then it suddenly occurred to me that I didn't know how we were going to get her out without my parents seeing her. I was lying in bed trying to figure that one out when Alex knocked on the door. I jumped out of the top bunk and clamped a hand over Phoebe's mouth. She didn't even open her eyes.

"Yes," I called out, trying to sound sleepy.

"We're going to have breakfast on Broadway. Want to come?"

Perfect. I could get her home while they were out. "No, thanks," I called. "You all go ahead."

"See you."

When I heard the front door close, I tried to wake her up. What a job. Phoebe sleeps soundly anyway, but on top of that she'd only had about five hours of sleep.

"Stop it, Miranda," she groaned. "Leave me alone."

"Phoebe, you've got to get up. I told my mother you were spending the night at your house. Now we have to get you home while they're out eating breakfast."

Well, she finally got the point and sat up. Then she groaned and fell back down on the pillow.

"My head hurts," she said.

"Were you drinking last night?"

She nodded and rolled back toward the wall.

"I'll get you some aspirin. Then you've got to get dressed."

It seemed to take forever, but she was finally up and dressed. I made her bed and steered her out to the dining room table.

"I've hidden your suitcase so we can pretend you just dropped over," I said. "You don't look as if you should go home just yet. How many drinks did you have?"

"Only two. But I guess they were pretty strong. And the music was loud with those twirling lights and mirrors."

"How could you have a drink? You're only thirteen," I asked.

"Philip got us the drinks. He had a fake I.D."

"Did you have a good time?"

"Oh, yes, it was great," she said brightly. "Philip is a terrific dancer." She wasn't looking at me, and I had this funny feeling that something wasn't right.

"Do you want something to eat?" I asked.

"Maybe just a piece of toast. My stomach feels sort of strange."

We didn't say anything as I walked around the kitchen fixing our breakfast. Suddenly, something was sitting between us that must have grown up from the lying and pretending we'd been doing. I wanted to say, "Why do you like that creepy guy?" and "Why do you smoke in front of him and do just what he wants you to do? If that's what liking boys is all about, you can count me out." But I didn't say any of it, and she sat there with her head on her hands staring out the window at the river.

Suddenly we heard the key in the lock.

"They're home. Remember, you just came over for breakfast."

She nodded.

When they walked into the kitchen, Michael Oliver was with them.

"Look who we found loitering around on the sidewalk," Alex said.

"Hello, Michael Oliver," I said. But he just nodded hello without looking at me. "This is Phoebe Livingston, Michael Oliver Westwater."

"Hi," Phoebe said.

"Had a hard night, Phoebe, old girl?" Alex said, clapping her on the back. Alex is always disgustingly cheery in the morning. It is one of his worst habits.

My father came in the room. "Miranda, I thought we might call Margaret and see if she would come to an impromptu meeting of the Save the Methodist Church Committee. The landmarks commission has put us on their schedule for this month, and we have a lot of work to do before then."

"Sure," I said. "Want to stay, Phoebe?"

"No, thanks," she said. "I've got to go running. See you later." She looked a little wavery on her feet, and I could see that my mother was watching her.

"Phoebe doesn't look very well this morning," she said to me when everybody else had gone into the living room.

I didn't answer.

"How's she getting along with her parents?" Mother asked.

"I guess everything is all right. She still goes to some psychiatrist over on the East Side, and she hates him. I have this feeling that Phoebe and her parents are never going to get along," I said.

"That happens," my mother said. I think both of us were thinking that we were glad it wasn't true in our family, but neither one of us said anything.

Margaret came up, and we sat around the living room, planning our strategy.

"The big thing about the landmarks hearing is that

we have to prove the building is unique architectur-ally," Pops said. "I think we ought to try and raise some money to hire an architectural historian. Dan Jordan says he's found a graduate student who will do the research and write up a report, but it will cost us about five hundred dollars."

"How about a raffle?" Margaret said. "I bet we could get some people to donate the prizes. Or maybe some of the businesses up on Broadway would be willing to contribute."

"Great idea," Michael Oliver said. He was taking notes, of course. I noticed that Alex was scribbling stuff down on his pad, too, but I knew he was taking notes on Michael Oliver.

They went on talking and making plans, but I tuned out. The adults had taken over and there wasn't much that Michael Oliver and I could add.

When the meeting was over, I decided to go for a walk in the park with Frisbee. "Do you want to come with me?" I asked Michael Oliver.

"No, thanks," he said. "Alex is going to show me how to lift weights."

"Oh, great," I said. "Another muscle man on the block." The two of them ignored me and went into Alex's room. It looked as if I had driven Michael Oliver into Alex's arms. Terrific.

I whistled for Frisbee, and we went out. It was cold, but I stayed out for a long time. I was trying to get away from everybody.

I didn't see Phoebe all week, and frankly I was just as glad. On the other hand, it looked as if Michael Oliver had moved in with us. I was staying late at the library in the afternoons, but whenever I got home, Michael Oliver was hanging out with Alex. He barely spoke to me, and I began to feel a little hurt. Finally, I cornered Alex one evening after Michael Oliver had left.

"How's your study going?" I asked from the door of his room. "It must be awfully convenient to have the subject dropping by every afternoon."

He didn't answer right away. He was scribbling away at his desk. I walked in and sat down on his bed.

"He's an interesting kid," Alex said.

"Aren't you feeling a little guilty about all this?" I asked. "That kid worships the ground you walk on, fool that he is, and the only reason you have him around is so you can 'study' him. What's going to happen when you hand in the paper? Are you going to drop him like a hot potato?"

In all my years of dealing with my brother, I'd never seen him look uncomfortable. But this time, I think I'd really hit the nail on the head.

"I don't know," he said, looking up at me. "What do you think I should do?"

"Rip up the paper and throw it away, or tell Michael Oliver what you're doing."

"He would run like a scared rabbit," he said.

"Maybe not, maybe he likes you enough." I

shrugged. "But you have to decide whether you like him enough. Michael Oliver needs friends and a place to go, and he's found it right here. To tell you the truth, I like him. I think he's lonely and a little strange, but his heart's in the right place. I don't want to see him hurt."

"So, Miss Righteous, why didn't you tell him right from the beginning what I was doing?"

"I guess I was hoping you'd give it up," I said.

We sat there in silence for a while. I got up and went into my own room. A little while later, I heard Alex turn on his radio really loud. That's his way of tuning out.

He came into my room just before I went to bed.

"I've been thinking about what you said. I've decided to write down my conclusions and turn the project in early. I'm cutting the whole thing short."

"I thought it was supposed to be a first semester project."

He shrugged. "I'll do something else instead."

I looked at him without answering. He knew what I was thinking.

"Miranda, it's December. I can't throw my notes out and start over again with someone else."

I turned away. "I don't care what you do," I said. He went out of my room and slammed the door behind him. That was mean of me. I know how guilty he felt because I felt the same way. Neither one of us wanted Michael Oliver to find out he was just a guinea pig.

Pops and Margaret went to the next block association meeting and got the community riled up about the church thing. It turned out that many members of the congregation did not want the church torn down either, and they were willing to work with us. The block association hired the student to do research on the architecture, and Margaret spent a lot of time trying to organize a petition drive. I agreed to go with her and some other people one evening at rush hour to catch people coming off the subway. Michael Oliver came too, and we worked together.

"You have to talk very fast," Margaret explained as we were walking down to Eighty-sixth Street. "These people are tired, they've worked a full day, and they want to get home and relax. You have to catch their interest quickly. Also, we want to try and sell them some raffle tickets, but the petitions come first. Ask them to sign only if they're residents of New York City and ask them to print their names clearly. We may want to call on them again later."

It was hard work. Someone had brought along a card table, and we put a big sign up that showed a picture of the Methodist church. Of course, it was pretty dark by five thirty, so it was hard to see. I was timid at first, and the people brushed past me, pretending they didn't hear me. I stopped to watch Margaret at work, and after a while I got the hang of it.

"Help us save the Methodist church," I yelled, running along beside a businessman. "Do you live in this neighborhood, sir? Please stop for just a minute and sign our petition."

"What are they doing to the church?" he asked, slowing down just a bit.

"They want to knock it down and build a high-rise building. You don't want Riverside Drive to look like Third Avenue, do you? We're asking the Landmarks Preservation Commission to designate the church a landmark and preserve it."

"All right, all right, I'll sign."

"I've got it," I said to Michael Oliver. "You bug them to death so the only way they'll get rid of you is to sign. Be sure each one takes a flyer."

He switched with me for a while, but he was so small nobody paid any attention to him so I took over the talking again. By six thirty, the stream of people had thinned out, and we decided to close up shop. I was exhausted and getting hoarse.

"How many signatures did we get?" I asked Margaret.

"It looks like about three hundred among the four corners. That's not bad, if they got the same number down on Seventy-ninth Street. We'll be out again the day after tomorrow if you two want to help us."

"Sure," I said.

"I have to go on ahead," Margaret said. "I have a meeting with some community people at seven."

"Want to stop at Baskin-Robbins?" I asked Michael Oliver.

"No, thanks. Alex convinced me to give up ice cream. I never realized it had so many chemicals."

"Michael Oliver, you've got to watch out for Alex. He's sort of fanatic on lots of subjects."

We turned down toward West End Avenue.

"You don't see what an amazing person he is, Miranda, because he's your brother. He knows so much about everything."

This was my chance to tell Michael Oliver the truth. "Do you know what Alex wants to be?" I asked.

He shook his head.

"He wants to be a psychologist. Do you know what that is?"

He nodded. "Don't worry, I know. The school called up my mother and told her I should go see somebody because I was withdrawn or something like that."

"What was it like?" I asked. I must say I didn't expect him to answer. He was such a secretive person.

"I hated it. He was this stupid man with a beard who kept asking dumb questions about my mother, and he made me draw pictures of things. The whole thing was ridiculous. Finally, Mom said I had to quit because it cost too much money. I told her I wasn't ever going back anyway, so that was that."

"Well, that's what Alex wants to do. Sit around all day and pry into other people's lives."

Michael Oliver glared at me. "He wouldn't ever do it that way. Alex would be the kind of person you could trust. I wouldn't mind telling him stuff because he'd know what to say."

I gave up right then and there. Michael Oliver wanted to believe that Alex was a saint, and nothing I said was going to change his mind.

When I got home the next day, there was a note by the phone that Phoebe had called.

"Want to go running?" she asked when I called her back.

"Sure. I'll meet you downstairs in ten minutes."

We ran for a long time without talking. Neither one of us had been out in a while, and it showed. We slowed down after two miles, and after three we gave up and walked.

"We're terrible," Phoebe said with a grin.

"Men and marathons don't mix. Confucius."

Her smile disappeared. "He hasn't called me, Miranda. Not since the disco night." She looked so sad I wanted to put my arm around her.

"He's probably been busy with exams or something," I said. It sounded lame.

"I keep wondering if it's something I did or said."

"Maybe it's your weird friend who doesn't drink or smoke and goes home right after the movie," I muttered.

She looked at me, but I could tell she hadn't heard. I whistled for Dungeon and Frisbee, who were almost out of sight.

"They didn't send Dungeon to New Jersey after all?" I said, trying to take her mind off her troubles.

"He goes next week," she said sadly. "The Fosters said I hadn't been walking him enough, and the baby is old enough to bug him now. I think they're scared Dungeon might bite her or something ridiculous."

"Did you ask your parents if you could keep him?"

"Yes. Of course they said no. No big surprise. Dad says my marks are too low, and I'm not concentrating —blah, blah, blah. The same old thing. Everything is always tied to my marks."

"I never told you the big news," I said suddenly. "Margaret and Grandpa are getting married."

"You're kidding," she screamed. "Why didn't you tell me? When did you find out?"

"A couple of weeks ago, I guess. I forgot, with everything else that's been going on. She's going to move to Vermont."

"That must make you sad. Sort of like me and Dungeon, but not exactly the same thing."

"No, Phoebe. Not quite," I said with a grin. "I don't know. I'm not as sad as I thought I'd be. She said I could come up for a whole month next summer.

She's going to rent the apartment, so she's not moving out forever. Maybe they'll come back sometime."

"Your grandfather will never come back to the city, Miranda. Don't kid yourself."

By that time we were back up by the Monument. "By the way, who is this Michael Oliver person?" Phoebe asked. "I saw him walking to Broadway with Alex the other day. What is this? Has your mother taken in boarders?"

"No, but I think if we gave him half the chance, he'd move in. I met him in the park this fall. He's sort of a weird, wonderful kid with a creepy family life. He lives in 345 and goes to the public school. He's the first one who figured out the Methodist church was going to sell. Right now, he's got a complete crush on Alex." We crossed the street and stopped again on the corner. "Do you want to come up?" I asked.

She hesitated. "I'd like to, but I keep thinking Philip might call. I guess I'll go home. Thanks anyway. See you."

I watched until she crossed the street. That run with Phoebe was just like old times. I realized how much I'd missed her lately. Secretly, I hoped Philip would drop out of her life. She wasn't her real self when she was with him. Besides, if he didn't keep asking her out, I wouldn't have to go on lying for her.

11 · Michael Oliver Finds Out

I got to the elevator door just as it opened. Michael Oliver was standing there, scribbling madly away in his notebook.

"Hi," I said.

He looked up at me with this sort of horrified expression on his face and tore off.

"Michael Oliver," I yelled, running after him. "What's wrong? What happened?"

By the time I caught up, he'd slipped through the inner door of his building and locked it behind him. For a second, he watched me banging on the glass door. Then he turned away and got into the elevator.

When I got home, Alex was in his room.

"What happened?"

He glanced at me. "He saw the report. I typed it last night and left it on my desk. For some crazy reason, Richard gave him the extra key from downstairs when nobody was home this afternoon, so Michael Oliver came up to wait for me and that's when he saw it."

I sat down on the bed. "Did you try to explain the whole thing? How you started out before either of us knew him at all?"

"He wouldn't listen to me." Alex's face looked white. "You know, he didn't cry or scream or anything. He just kept saying he couldn't believe that we would do this to him. The last thing he said was, 'You make me feel like a monkey in the zoo. I thought you wanted to be my friend.' " Alex put his head down on his arms. It must have been awful. All our worst dreams come true.

"I guess you couldn't have pretended the report was about somebody else," I said.

"Read it," he said, handing me the pile of papers. "I don't give him a name but he's unmistakably Michael Oliver Westwater."

I took the report and went into my own room to read it. First it gave a whole list of the days and times the "subject" had been observed. Then came the detailed notes on the subject's behavior. At the end, there was a list of conclusions and suggested treatment for the subject. Actually, if the thing hadn't been about Michael Oliver, I would have been pretty impressed. Maybe Alex was going into the right business.

"Miranda, come here," Alex called.

I went back into his room. "Look," he said, pointing out the window. Michael Oliver had hung a big sign out his window. It read: THE ZOO IS CLOSED FOR THE DAY.

"I feel terrible," I said.

"So do I. What are we going to do?" Alex said.

"I don't know. Let's just think about it for a while."

The two of us wandered around the apartment like zombies. Dinner was silent, and no matter what subject they brought up, Mother and Pops couldn't get a rise out of either of us. They finally gave up.

The phone rang, and Alex and I both jumped. "I'll get it," I said.

It was Phoebe. "Miranda, is that you?" She was whispering.

"Yes," I said dully.

"Philip just called me. He wants me to meet him on Broadway in twenty minutes. Can I tell my parents I'm coming to your place?"

I was silent for a long time.

"Miranda, are you still there?" she said. "It's all right, isn't it?"

"No, it's not all right," I said finally. "I'm just not going to cover up for anybody anymore."

"You're kidding," she said with this note of fury in her voice. "You must be kidding. I thought you were my best friend. I'm just asking you to do this one thing for me. Come on, Miranda." She was back to pleading again. "I'm sure they're not going to check up on me. He just wants to meet me at the coffee shop to talk."

"I won't blow the whistle on you, Phoebe, but I warn you if they call, I'm going to tell the truth, that you're not here." My voice sounded shaky.

"Great friend," she spat into the phone and slammed it down.

I ran to my room, jumped into bed, and burst into tears.

I lay there in the dark for a long time. Finally, someone knocked gently on the door and pushed it open. It was Mother.

"Are you all right, Miranda?" she asked.

Just the sound of her voice made me start crying all over again.

She sat down beside me and began to rub my back the way she used to when I had asthma.

"Do you want to talk about what's wrong?" she asked.

"I don't know. I'm keeping a lot of secrets, and they're beginning to get to me."

Neither one of us said anything for a while. Mother never pries. She doesn't think it's fair. After a while, I sat up.

"Phoebe's parents don't know she's going out with this guy, Philip. She keeps telling them she's coming over here, and I cover for her. Then tonight, she called and asked me to do it again and I said no, I wasn't going to, and she slammed the phone down, and I guess she's never going to speak to me again."

Mother started to say something, but I stopped her. "That's not all. I might as well tell you every-thing. You know the project Alex has been working on where he's supposed to observe somebody and do a report on them?"

She nodded.

"Well, do you know who he's been observing?"

She shook her head.

"Michael Oliver."

"Oh no," she said. "And Michael Oliver didn't know it?"

"Not until today. Richard gave him the key so he could wait for us here, and he saw the report on Alex's desk."

"But that's such a cruel thing for Alex to do," Mother said. "It doesn't sound like him."

"Well, Alex started watching Michael Oliver last fall when he used to sit on the fire escape. That was before either of us knew him. Than I met him in the park one day and a couple of weeks later, I figured out that Michael Oliver was Alex's subject. I didn't tell either of them. That was wrong of me, I guess, but I just kept hoping Alex would give up the project. Anyway, things got worse because Michael Oliver met Alex and got a crush on him, and neither one of us could stand to tell Michael Oliver what Alex was really doing. And Alex didn't want to give up the study because he had put so much work into it. It's a mess."

"But still, Alex should never have gone on with the study without asking Michael Oliver's permission. I'm going to have to speak to Alex about this."

"He feels pretty rotten already, Mother. It was my fault just as much as his. He had gone ahead and finished up the report early. That's why Michael Oliver saw it on his desk, and the whole thing blew up in our faces." I paused. "I think that's why I finally said no to Phoebe tonight. After I saw what happened with Michael Oliver, I decided I wasn't going to cover up for anybody anymore. I'm sick of being in the middle of all these things."

"I don't blame you," Mother said. "It's a horrible position to be in, and it usually comes from not being able to say no to people. Do you think Phoebe's parents would let her go out with Philip if she told them the truth?"

I shrugged. "She thinks they'd have a fit. I guess I believe her. But it seems like a vicious circle. It's terrible they don't trust her. But when you see what she does, why should they, really?"

Mother nodded. "Maybe there's some way you could tell Phoebe that. She would probably accept advice from you that she wouldn't be able to take from her parents."

"Not anymore," I said glumly. "I don't think she'll ever speak to me again."

Mother gave me a little hug. "Don't worry, Miranda. She'll get over this."

We were silent for a long time. "Phoebe changes when she's with Philip. I hope that doesn't happen to me when I go out with boys."

"It's very important to Phoebe that people like her. Maybe it has something to do with her having been adopted."

The phone rang out in the kitchen. "Alex will get it," I said. "We both keep hoping Michael Oliver will call."

Alex came down the hall. "Miranda, it's Mrs. Livingston. She asked for Phoebe, and when I said she wasn't here, she asked to speak to you."

Mother looked at me. "Phoebe must have thought you'd cover for her anyway."

I went to the phone. "Hello," I said.

"Miranda, is Phoebe on her way home?" Mrs. Livingston asked. "I told her she could only come over for a little while."

I took a deep breath. "Phoebe hasn't been here, Mrs. Livingston. I haven't seen her since this afternoon."

"How strange," she said. "I thought she said she was coming over to your place. I wonder if she could have taken Dungeon out. Well, thank you, Miranda. Sorry to bother you."

"It's all right. Good-bye," I said quietly and hung up.

"What happened?" Mother asked, coming up behind me.

"She wanted Phoebe to come home. I told her Phoebe wasn't here, but I didn't tell her where Phoebe'd gone."

"Where did she go?"

"Philip wanted to meet her on Broadway at a coffee shop." I glanced at the clock. "She called at the end of dinner, so that must have been about eight o'clock, and said she was supposed to meet him in twenty minutes. It's ten now. I wonder what she's doing?"

"Come on, Miranda," Mother said. She pulled our coats out of the closet. "We're going to tell Phoebe that her mother is looking for her. We'll give her the chance to tell the truth herself."

"What if we can't find her?" I asked.

"Then you'll have to call Mrs. Livingston and tell her where Phoebe went."

I nodded, but I felt sick inside.

The wind was whipping around the corner of our building so we were blown halfway to Broadway.

Mother stayed outside the door while I went inside the coffee shop. Philip and Phoebe were sitting in the corner. They were holding hands, but they pulled away from each other when I came up.

"Hello," Philip said in the most unwelcoming voice I've ever heard.

"Miranda, what are you doing here?" Phoebe said. She sounded worried.

"Your mother called my house. She was looking for you."

"Oh, no. What did you tell her?"

"I said I hadn't seen you since this afternoon."

Phoebe started pulling on her coat. "I can't believe you did that," she muttered.

"I told you I wasn't going to lie for you anymore, Phoebe," I said. I felt as if my stomach was going to cave in. "I really meant it."

"Well, Miss Goody Two Shoes, did you tell her where I was?"

I shook my head. "Look, Phoebe, why don't you just take Philip in and introduce him to your parents. It would be much better than this lying and hiding."

She didn't answer.

"I'll walk you home," Philip said.

As they headed out the door, Phoebe turned back to me. "Hey, Miranda, will you do me a favor?" she called.

"Sure, Phoebe," I said. "What is it?"

"Drop dead."

Mother was waiting for me outside. She put her arm around my shoulders when she saw the miserable look on my face.

"I saw them leave," she said. "But they didn't see me. I figured that would make things worse." She steered me over to the entrance of Baskin-Robbins. "Come on. A little chocolate almond fudge can work wonders."

To be honest, I didn't feel like any ice cream but I agreed. We sat and ate our cones and walked slowly home.

When we got to Michael Oliver's building, I went inside to look at the list of names by the buzzers. Mother came up behind me.

"What are you doing?" she asked.

"Trying to figure out which one is Michael Oliver. His mother took back her maiden name so the apartment's not listed under Westwater."

"What floor is he on?"

"It must be the sixth because that's where he was sitting on the fire escape.

I ran my finger down the names.

"He's in the back so it's probably not the A line. Maybe 6C or D."

"Don't buzz up now, Miranda," Mother said. "It's too late."

"I won't. I'll bring Alex with me. We'll do it tomorrow afternoon."

12 • Dr. Bartlett Proves Himself

Phoebe didn't call me the next day. I was dying to know what had happened, but I knew I couldn't call her. I figured she never wanted to see me again.

Around tea time, I rang Margaret's doorbell. When she saw who it was, she had a huge smile on her face.

"Miranda, you're just the person I want to see."

"Boy, that's the nicest thing I've heard in weeks," I said. "What's up?"

"Well, your grandfather and I've decided to get married in the middle of January in Vermont, and we want you and Alex to be in the wedding."

"Whoopee," I screamed and threw my arms around her. "I've always wanted to be a bridesmaid. It's especially nice that I can be yours."

"Now come on," she said, pulling her coat out of the closet. "We're going to the material store. I want to make your dress."

So off we went to Broadway, chattering all the way. Margaret was full of plans. "We're going to be married in the living room with a minister and just our closest friends and family. I want to ask Phoebe too. Do you think she'll come?"

"I'm not sure," I said. "Phoebe and I had a fight last night. I don't think she wants to have anything to do with me."

"What happened, Miranda?"

I poured out the whole story. She didn't say anything for a long time after I finished. That's just like Margaret. She really thinks about what you're telling her.

"You were caught in the middle, weren't you?" she said. "Sometimes it's hard to be a good friend. It means you have to make choices all the time."

"I miss Phoebe," I said. "Ever since she met Philip, things have been different. I guess I went along with whatever she wanted because I wanted to keep her as my friend." We stopped at the curb and waited for the light. "I don't think she'll ever speak to me again."

"If she's a true friend, she will," Margaret said. "Now let's think about something else. What's your favorite color?"

We spent a long time poring over the patterns and materials. Finally, we decided on a blue velvet skirt. Margaret insisted on buying everything. "This is my present," she said. When we got home, she asked me to stay for tea, but I said no. "I'd better get upstairs to walk Frisbee. I've been neglecting her lately."

Alex was waiting for me. "Where've you been?" he asked. When I started to tell him, he interrupted. "Never mind. Now listen, we've got to talk to Michael Oliver. I couldn't get anything done at school thinking about him. Besides, Mother had a little talk with me this morning." He gave me this look as if to say why'd you spill the beans, but I didn't say anything.

"Knowing Michael Oliver, he's going to squirrel himself away and pour everything into that notebook, and that isn't healthy. We've got to have it out with him. It would be better for all of us."

"I stopped by his lobby yesterday. I figure he must live in the back on the sixth floor. Why don't we go ring the bells and see who answers?"

"You're on. Let's go."

So poor Frisbee was abandoned yet again while we carried out our plan. No one answered the first bell we rang. The second one, some lady answered who'd never heard of Michael Oliver. The third one, Michael Oliver answered.

"It's him," Alex said, putting his hand over the intercom.

"Tell him to come down to sign for a package, I whispered. "He'll never come if he knows it's us."

"UPS," Alex said. "You have to sign for something."

"We didn't order anything," Michael Oliver said. That kid wasn't dumb.

"You have to sign, mister," Alex said.

"Oh, all right," he said, after a pause. "I'll be right down."

We hid on either side of the inner door so he couldn't see us through the glass. My heart was beating so hard I felt it was in my head. Finally, the door opened slowly.

Alex jumped out and grabbed him by the arm. "Hi, Michael Oliver," he said. "We want to talk to you."

"I knew there was something fishy. We never get packages." He tried to pull away from Alex. "I don't want to talk to you guys. You can go have your fun studying some other poor sucker."

"Michael Oliver, we came over to say we were sorry," I said quickly. "You should at least hear us out. It's not as bad as you think."

"I bet," he said, but he stopped trying to get away from Alex.

"Come to our place," Alex said. "It's too cold to stand here and talk."

Michael Oliver didn't answer for a minute. He was looking at our faces, trying to figure out if this was just another trick.

"Please come over and let us explain," I said. "We wouldn't have come looking for you if we didn't care."

"All right, I'll come for a minute," he said. "But you

can let go of me now. I'm not going to run away."
Alex let him go, and the three of us trudged next door
without saying a word. In fact, we didn't say one
thing to each other until we were in our kitchen.
Michael Oliver sat down in the chair by the window.
He was going to let us do the talking. Alex started.

"This whole thing has been my fault. I was given
this assignment as a special honors project. I had to
study one person and write down everything I observed. One day, I looked out the window and there
you were sitting on your fire escape, scribbling away
in your notebook, and I thought, how perfect. You
were nearby, and I could see into your living room
and part of your kitchen. That meant I didn't have to
pick a friend or a member of the family—"

"Thank the Lord," I said. Michael Oliver smiled
for just a second.

"—and I was pretty sure I could watch you easily,
just by looking out my window. The trouble was it
began to get cold and you stopped coming out on the
fire escape. In November, my observations dwindled
down to nothing. Subject went through the kitchen
at five P.M. Stuff like that. I was getting desperate.
Then I walked into our kitchen one day, and you
were sitting at the table with Miranda."

"Now let me tell my side of it," I interrupted. "You
remember the day we met in the park?"

He nodded.

"Do you remember what you said to me?"

He looked out the window again.

"You said, 'That's the first time you've done ten laps.' You were talking about my running." I paused. Michael Oliver was still staring out the window. "Now you must have been 'studying' me pretty well to have known that. Alex isn't the only one who's been watching people."

"I wasn't going to tell anybody. I wasn't going to hand in some paper on you to my teacher. You weren't going to be my 'subject,'" Michael Oliver yelled. Then he burst into tears. Alex and I were stunned.

I sat down beside him and put my arm around him. "Michael Oliver, the reason we dragged you here is because we like you, and we don't want to lose you as a friend."

"We're really sorry all this happened," Alex said.

Michael Oliver pulled away and rubbed at his tears. I think he was mad he'd cried in front of us.

"When I first met you, I didn't know you were the person Alex was studying. I didn't figure that out until a couple of weeks ago. I kept hoping Alex would finish his project and the whole thing would be over with."

We were silent for a minute. There didn't seem to be anything more to say.

"We wanted to tell you how we felt, Michael Oliver. It was hard for us to do this. Sometimes I just want to hide all my feelings in a notebook too. But that just hurts worse later," Alex said softly.

Michael Oliver stood up. "Are you finished?" he asked. Alex and I looked at each other.

"I guess so," I said.

"I've got to get home," he mumbled, looking at his shoes. "I'll see you."

We sat there listening to him walking down the hall. The door closed softly behind him.

"I kept thinking he'd talk to us, tell us how he felt," I said with a sigh.

"You can't expect him to change overnight," Alex said. "Who knows? He might be back."

"You were great, Alex," I said as I stood up. "Maybe you are in the right profession."

He didn't answer.

When you've got trouble, it's nice to know you and your brother are on the same side of the fence.

That's one of the things I learned that afternoon.

I think it was the next day that Michael Oliver started putting the signs up in the window. The first one said, I'M STILL MAD.

"Isn't that perfect?" Alex said as we stood looking at it. "He's telling us how he feels. He's just not ready to say it to our faces."

That sign stayed up for a couple of days. The next one said, THANKS ALEX.

"What does that mean?" I asked.

"I sent him the paper," Alex said. He was sitting at his desk.

"You're kidding. What about the honors project?"

"The teacher said if I could get something in by the end of January, he wouldn't flunk me on it." He swung around in his chair. "Now sit down, Miss Bartlett, and tell me how you're feeling today."

"Oh no," I said, backing out of the room. "Not me. I'll see you February first. I'm going on a long trip."

Alex laughed. "It's all right. My friend Peter said I could study him. He couldn't care less. That's just what I need. A nice healthy subject."

The next time I went running, Michael Oliver was walking out of his building.

"Hi," I said. "Want to see how many laps I get done today?"

He blushed. "No, thanks. What's happened on the church?"

"They had the commission hearing yesterday. Margaret and Pops went along with some people from the block association. Pops said it went very well. They were impressed with the research we'd done. But the commission won't decide for a couple of months."

Michael Oliver nodded. "Is Alex upstairs?"

"Sure," I said, as I jogged away. "Go on up."

13 · The Wedding

A week had gone by since I'd seen Phoebe, and I was still feeling rotten about her. I went to Woolworth's and bought her a pedometer for Christmas. That's a thing that you hook on your waistband so you can see how far you've run. I remembered she'd said she wanted one last summer but she never got it. I wrapped it up and left it with the doorman of her building.

We were celebrating Christmas at home. Sometimes we go to Vermont, but this year Grandpa was coming to New York so he could see Margaret and us at the same time. Mother and I spent one whole day decorating the apartment, and it looked really beautiful Christmas Eve. The only thing missing was a fireplace, but Alex and I had gotten used to hanging our stockings on the radiator cover.

Christmas morning, Alex woke me up. "Come into

my room," he said. "Michael Oliver has struck again."

There was a big sign in his window that read MERRY CHRISTMAS, BARTLETTS.

"Let's make one for ours," I said. We scurried around and found green and red Magic Markers and a big piece of cardboard. When we finished, it was time for breakfast and stockings. My favorite present was the blue velvet skirt. Margaret laughed when I gave her a hug. "I stayed up most of the night finishing it," she said. "I haven't put the hooks on yet."

After lunch, we went for a walk through the park. Lots of other people were out too.

"I wonder what kind of day Michael Oliver is having," I said to Alex.

"I was thinking the same thing." He glanced at me. "Where's Phoebe? I haven't seen her in ages."

"Don't ask, Dr. Bartlett. It's a long story."

"I figured something had happened. Man trouble?"

"Sort of. With me in the middle."

"Why don't you ring her doorbell on our way home? She's probably had too much of family Christmas."

I laughed. "Ringing people's doorbells seems to be your solution to everything." But it wasn't a bad idea.

The doorman called up for me.

"Go on up," he said.

"Did you talk to Phoebe Livingston?"

He shrugged. "Whoever answered said for you to come up."

I had second thoughts in the elevator. What was I going to say to her? Or to Mrs. Livingston, for that matter?

Phoebe opened the door. "Hello," she said.

"Hi, I just thought I'd come up and wish you Merry Christmas."

"Come in," she said. "I'm all alone. My parents went to some party on the East Side. I didn't want to go, so I pretended to be sick."

She led me back to her room, and we sat down on her bed. Nobody said anything for a minute, and I began to wish I hadn't come.

"Thanks for the pedometer," she said after a while. "That was a really nice present."

"You're welcome." I looked around the room. "What else did you get?"

"Oh, the usual. Some of those old-fashioned dresses from Mom. The ones with the smocking that people stopped wearing about twenty years ago. My parents never learn. She did give me some nail polish, though. Look at it." She held out her hands.

"It's pretty. My nails are too ugly for that stuff."

Another silence. We were both trying to decide what to say next. Finally, I started.

"I'm sorry about not covering for you. I just didn't

want to lie anymore. I'm not good at it and one lie kept leading to another."

Phoebe was staring out the window. "It doesn't matter. Mother was waiting in the lobby, and she saw Philip, so the whole thing blew up anyway."

"What did she say?"

"Just what I expected. How could I have betrayed her? I was too young to go out with boys, why hadn't I invited him to meet them, and so on. I'm grounded now. No running, no going out without them." She shrugged. "Pretty soon Mother will start picking me up at school as if I'm six years old."

"Really?"

"I'm kidding, Miranda. But she might as well. If I'm not home at four o'clock, she starts calling the school."

"What about Philip?"

"He wrote me a letter saying he couldn't hassle this thing with my parents and he'd see me in a couple of years. Nice guy."

Poor Phoebe. It sounded as if the world had fallen in on her.

"And to top it all off, Dungeon's gone. The Fosters sent him to New Jersey last week."

"Oh, Phoebe," I said.

She was still staring out the window but I saw these two tears rolling down her cheek. I moved over next to her and put my arm around her shoulder.

"Things are going to get better, you'll see. Pretty

soon, your parents will loosen up and you'll meet lots of boys."

"I hate them," she sobbed. "I feel like running away again. Maybe I should go out and try to find my real mother. I bet she's wonderful."

I'm too shy to be very good at this comforting stuff, but I had to keep trying.

"Phoebe, I know your parents love you, and they're just trying to do the right thing. What if you just gave them a chance?"

"What do you mean?"

"Why don't you give them one month and do exactly what they want. Pull up your marks, don't go out without permission, wear a skirt to dinner without complaining. The whole thing." She was rolling her eyes. "Wait a minute. Just hear me out. Then at least you three wouldn't waste your time arguing about the same things, and you could tell them how you feel about them not trusting you. Maybe they would start trusting you again."

She didn't say anything for a minute. "It would make them think they'd won," she said.

"You three are not supposed to be fighting a war," I answered. "Look, you're not going to get out of this house for five more years! Why not make the next five years peaceful ones?" If only my mother could hear me now, I thought. She'd die.

"Your parents are great people, Miranda. You don't know what it's like to live with mine."

I nodded. "I didn't say it was going to be easy."

"I'll think about it," she said, but I couldn't tell what she'd decide.

I got up to go. "I guess you can't even come over to our place. Alex got one of those electronic games from Grandpa. It's really fun."

She shook her head. "No way."

"Did Margaret talk to you?"

"I haven't seen anybody," she said.

"She's getting married on January fifteenth in Vermont, and she wants you to come. We're driving up and you could come with us."

For the first time, Phoebe smiled. "That'd be fun," she said. "I'll have to see what my jailers say."

"I'll see you," I said, pulling on my coat. "Let me know when you can go running again. Frisbee and I are getting pretty lonely out there without you."

"Thanks," she said. "I will."

The wedding was beautiful. Phoebe's parents did let her come after all, and we drove up the day before. Grandpa and Margaret were waiting for us so we sat down to a huge dinner, complete with candles and wine.

Everybody toasted everybody else and Margaret looked pretty and so perfect for Grandpa that I got this silly lump in my throat. We went to bed really late. Phoebe and I were staying in the cottage.

"They look happy," Phoebe said. "It must be nice to fall in love again when you're old."

"I never think of Margaret as old," I answered. I put my hands up to my cheeks. They were hot. "Do I look red?"

"Yes," Phoebe said with a grin. "How many glasses of wine did you drink?

"Only one and a half." I collapsed on the bed. "We'd better get to sleep. I don't want to be a hungover bridesmaid."

I was almost asleep when she said something.

"What, Phoebe?" I mumbled.

"I said I'm trying what you told me and it might even work."

"Great," I said. It wasn't until the next day I figured out she was talking about her parents.

There were only twenty-five people at the wedding. Pops gave Margaret away, and Alex and I stood beside them in front of the fireplace. The service was very short and afterwards we had lunch on our laps in the living room. Alex plunked down beside me.

"Aren't you having any wine, Miranda?" he asked.

I groaned. "I'm just getting over last night. Don't talk to me about wine."

"They look great together, don't they?" Alex said. Margaret and Grandpa were standing in front of the fireplace.

"Yup. But I can't believe Margaret won't be coming home with us tomorrow."

Alex raised his glass. "I have a toast to make," he said. "Just for us. Here's to Michael Oliver Westwater and the Methodist church and Margaret and Grandpa and Phoebe coming back. Does that cover everything, Miss Bartlett?"

"Yes, Dr. Bartlett," I said with a grin. "That does cover everything."